Tessa
Masterson
Will Go
to Prom

Also by Emily Franklin & Brendan Halpin

Jenna & Jonah's Fauxmance

Tessa Masterson Will Go to Prom

Emily Franklin &
Brendan Halpin

Walker & Company ✹ New York

First published in the United States of America in March 2012
by Walker Publishing Company, Inc., a division of Bloomsbury Publishing, Inc.
www.bloomsburyteens.com

For information about permission to reproduce selections from this book, write to
Permissions, Walker BFYR, 175 Fifth Avenue, New York, New York 10010

Library of Congress Cataloging-in-Publication Data
Franklin, Emily.
Tessa Masterson will go to prom / by Emily Franklin and Brendan Halpin.
p.   cm.
Summary: Feeling humiliated and confused when his best friend Tessa rejects his love
and reveals a long-held secret, high school senior Luke must decide if he should stand
by Tessa when she invites a female date to the prom, sparking a firestorm
of controversy in their small Indiana town.
ISBN 978-0-8027-2345-1
[1. Best friends—Fiction.   2. Friendship—Fiction.   3. Lesbians—Fiction.   4. Proms—
Fiction.   5. Indiana—Fiction.]   I. Halpin, Brendan.   II. Title.
PZ7.F8583Te 2012   [Fic]—dc23   2011025042

Book design by DDesigns
Typeset by Westchester Book Composition
Printed in the U.S.A. by Quad/Graphics, Fairfield, Pennsylvania
2 4 6 8 10 9 7 5 3 1

*For my children—may you love deeply and be loved openly
And for Papa, who loved me unconditionally —E. F.*

For Kerr Griffin and Melissa Kappotis —B. H.

Tessa
Masterson
Will Go
to Prom

1

⋈

Tessa

Before you read the paper or watch tonight's news, before you grab the *Time* magazine in your orthodontist's office or dig into the police report, before the protesters' shouts distract you, you should hear the whole thing from the beginning. Of course, you can't go to the very beginning, because that'd probably take you back to when I was born and you'd have to see me learn to walk, mumble my first word ("apple," for those taking notes), and watch me ditch the training wheels and pedal right into Lucas Fogelman—smiling from the side of his mouth. And you'd have to know about Lucas being an All-State pitcher and how maybe he'll make it to the majors, or maybe just the Indianapolis Indians or the South Bend Silver Hawks. And you'd know about my scholarship to Northwestern and that I wrote my college essay about how I go running when I'm nervous. But all those details, the ones in essays or in the newspapers, the bits and pieces of us dredged up in interviews ("She always seemed so normal to me!"), the best article in the world won't tell you everything. We will.

2

LUKE

I think I've seen too many chick flicks. Mom loves them, and our house is not that big, so there's no real way to escape them.

Okay, it's not really a house. It's an apartment over Hailer's Drugstore. Or, it was over Hailer's Drugstore before the MegaMart on Route 126 drove Hailer's out of business. Now it's an apartment over an empty space.

10 Things I Hate About You. The Wedding Singer. Lots of romantic comedies involve the guy making some big, over-the-top public display where he sings a song or something and reveals his love for the girl, and she melts into his arms. I'm not much of a singer, but I do have access to a lighted sign.

There were two events that got me thinking. One

was in Jenny Himmelrath's basement. The other was in Tessa's.

It was a Sunday afternoon and Jenny and I had gone to the lake because there's really not much else to do around here. "I'm starving. You want to come back to my house for a snack?" she asked.

I did not say, "Well, we damn sure can't go back to my house because it's actually an apartment over an empty storefront and even though Mom cleans like a fiend we can't quite get rid of the mice and it's just embarrassing all the way around." Though I could have said that to Tessa. And she would have laughed and offered to bring her brother's BB gun to see if we could pick off some mice. Instead, I said, "Sure. Sounds great!"

We went back to Jenny's house. Her parents were at an all-day church committee meeting, so the house was empty. She put on some music. It was Miss Kaboom's "Shake It." Too fast to be make-out music, but, then again, definitely a song about the pleasure of moving your body. I wondered if maybe Jenny was going to test the limits of what you can get away with and still wear one of those purity rings.

And she might have, if I hadn't gotten a text from Tessa right after we'd drained our sodas and there was an awkward pause. The kind of awkward pause you're supposed to fill with a kiss. It filled with my phone buzzing.

Which wouldn't have been that bad if I hadn't whipped it out—my phone, I mean—to answer the text. It wasn't even anything important. It was just some random thing she'd thought of, but I just never leave Tessa hanging because she's my best friend.

I put my phone away and turned to Jenny, who was staring at me.

"Um. What?" I said.

"What? *What?* Wow, Luke, I can't even believe I was going to risk hell for you." I would like to point out that I did not giggle when she said that.

"I'm sorry, Jenny, but I don't know what you're talking about."

"I'm talking about—you know, Luke, you have this reputation for being a nice guy, but you're not a nice guy. You're a jerk. You're a jerk to every girl you date because you're in love with someone else, and you're probably a jerk to her too because she obviously loves you and you don't even know it. How many other guys has she dated? Oh, that's right, none. She's waiting for you to open your dumb eyes."

"What are you even talking about?"

Jenny rose from the couch and looked at me. "Wow. That's just pathetic. You really—you don't know. You really think you and Tessa are just friends. It probably never occurred to you to wonder why she doesn't have a boyfriend. Or why you can't keep a girlfriend. Luke, get out of my basement and go see your *real* girlfriend, Tessa."

Okay, so that was one thing that got me thinking.

The other one happened the following Friday. I wasn't going out with Jenny, and Tessa, as Jenny pointed out, did not have a boyfriend. So after my baseball game I went over to her house to watch movies like we've done a million times before.

She popped in *The Philadelphia Story*, which I'd never seen. I don't usually like black-and-white movies anyway, but this was one of those movies about two people who don't think they're in love but actually are. (In this movie they were exes, but whatever.)

Was she sending me a message? Why'd she pick that movie? I was wondering this stuff while pretending to pay attention to the movie when Tessa got tired and stretched out on the couch with her head in my lap.

Well, technically her head was resting on my right thigh. If it had been all the way in my lap, she might have found it kind of . . . uncomfortable.

I mean, Jenny Himmelrath with her stupid purity ring and all, might have been right. Tessa was sending me a pretty clear signal. Right? You don't just put your head in someone's lap without that meaning something.

And then Tessa said this: "I just love Katharine Hepburn in this movie. She's like tough and fragile at the same time. I totally want to be her." She paused for a minute. "Or, you know, make out with her." I laughed at her joke, and then she laughed, but then I thought about it. Tessa wanted to be Katharine Hepburn, whose character was pretending not to be in love with someone she was actually in love with. Tessa really was practically hitting me over the head with it.

I started noticing how much Tessa touched me. Every touch on the forearm, every squeeze of the shoulder, every poke in the ribs, everything that I had stupidly just written off as something people who've been best friends since childhood do suddenly made sense in a different way.

And I realized that Jenny wasn't just right about Tessa—she was right about me, too.

Mom picked up on this with her scary mom radar. I wasn't seeing her much—Tessa's parents, the Mastersons, promoted Mom to manager of the store bakery, which meant she had to be at work at four thirty every morning. Which meant she was in bed by nine at the latest. Nights when we had away games, I didn't see her at all.

So I came home one Tuesday afternoon after practice and sat down at the kitchen table, drinking a sports drink. Mom just stared at me.

"Who is she?" she said from the sink as she scrubbed a plate.

"Who is who?" I said.

"The girl you're obsessing about. Don't just sit there, help me dry." She tossed a dish towel at me, and I got up and started drying.

"I'm not obsessing about anybody," I lied as I put a plate away.

"Liar. You just got home from practice and did not eat two thousand calories' worth of anything. So who is she?"

I dried out the big plastic cup we'd gotten at a Cincinnati Reds game last summer and figured telling the truth would be easier than trying to deflect her questions for the next hour and a half. "I . . . I think she's Tessa," I said almost in a whisper.

Mom laughed. "Well, thank God! The whole town's been waiting for you guys to make it official for years. And Tessa's a good kid with good parents. I worry like hell about you dating those purity-ring girls. Those girls get a third date with a boy, they wind up pregnant. That is something you do not need, and I am way too young to be a grandmother. I'm sure Tessa at least knows what a condom is."

"Agh, Mom, God!"

"Don't Mom-God me. You come home with a pregnant girlfriend before you've got a bachelor's degree in your hand and I'll—"

"Cut off my man parts and feed them to me. I know, Mom, you've said the same damn thing every time I've left the house to do anything except play baseball. You need a new line." I think she's probably joking about mutilating me, but I'm not a hundred percent sure.

Mom was one of those churchy girls who didn't know anything about sex when she, valedictorian of Brookfield-Mason Regional High, went off to Purdue. And she was one of those girls who got pregnant on her third date. She didn't even finish her freshman year. So she's been pretty adamant about me not fathering a kid until I've got a degree. And my getting a full ride to Purdue to play baseball has only made her more freaky about this.

"Fine," Mom said. "You know what, if you're with Tessa, I'm not going to worry. That girl's got enough sense for the both of you. And I like her family."

When Mom came back to Brookfield pregnant, the Mastersons gave her a job, "which is more than any of those holier-than-thou sons of bitches at First Lutheran ever offered a girl in need," according to my mom.

"Well, great, Mom. I'm glad you approve," I said. "Now what do we have to eat in this dump, anyway?" That earned me a pretty hard punch in the arm. "Hey, not the pitching arm, Mom, okay?"

"Toughen up, Sally," Mom said, laughing.

—————

So I was on board and, according to Mom and Jenny Himmelrath, the whole town was on board too. That just left Tessa.

I thought about different ways to do it. There was the classic lean in for a kiss in her basement, but I felt like I wanted it to be bigger than that. If she'd really been waiting for me while I went through a bunch of Jenny Himmelraths at Brookfield-Mason Regional (or BM, as our sports opponents never tire of calling it), then I owed her something a little bigger. Larger scale.

Of course the whole town was going to find out anyway—everybody in Brookfield knows if you've taken a dump before you even have a chance to flush—but I thought it would be cool to tell the whole town how I felt.

And I figured Prom would be a great place for us to come out as a couple. In Indiana, you've got the basketball tournament, the Indianapolis 500, Notre Dame football, and the Prom. I couldn't really involve Tessa in any of the first three, so it was going to have to be the Prom.

It was crazy in so many ways: if it didn't work, I was risking a lifelong friendship; you don't start dating someone at the end of senior year, especially if you're going to colleges two and a half hours apart in the fall; and putting up a twenty-foot-tall sign about your feelings is just not something guys usually do.

But I've seen enough chick flicks to know that anything that feels this crazy must be love.

3

Tessa

It's easy for me to know what everyone wants. The guy walking up to the counter, he'll want a refund on his $5.99 sandwich. Too soggy—I can see the mustard leaking into the white paper wrapper. The mother with her whining twins doesn't know whether to complain to me about how small our ice cream portions are or deal with the fact that her kids are making a puddle of mint chocolate chip on the floor that someone—me, probably—will have to clean up.

"How can I help you?" I ask the sandwich guy even though I already know the answer.

I've always found it simple, really, to look in to someone's eyes, study how they're standing—shoulders up, chin-out angry, or hunched-over worried—and figure out what they need. My parents pride themselves on the Five Steps of Customer Satisfaction, which is the backbone of both of their Giant Brookfield Markets. The name is sort of a joke if you're at all familiar with Brookfield, Indiana, because we are *so* not a giant town. But my parents figured that a name is a selling point; if you call something giant, people will believe it. And it's worked so far.

Giant Brooks, as the stores are affectionately known, is one of the biggest employers around here, and I count myself among the employees, my blue plastic name tag pinned to my regulation collared shirt. Then there are the khaki pants my mother always wants me to belt, but which I insist on wearing a little too low for her tastes.

"What's the point of serving me a sandwich I can't eat?" Sandwich Guy complains.

"I hear you," I tell Sandwich Guy, because the first step in customer satisfaction is to listen. Then I go to step two, the apology: "I'm so sorry for your trouble!" Cue my bright smile and reassuring gaze.

"What're you gonna do to help?" he asks, shoving the crinkled lunch bag in my face. From the corner of my eye I can see Lucas standing and waving from under the FRESH COFFEE ROASTERS sign near the baked goods section. I wonder why he's here before my shift is over, but I grin and try to ignore him to focus on the task at hand. Step three always feels the best: solve the issue.

"How about we refund your money and give you a new country-ham-and-provolone on the house?" This seems to satisfy the guy and he nods as though he's won a huge battle instead of the six bucks he spent on our deli sandwich. "Thanks so much for your patience," I say to him while Lucas does some jumping jacks to get my attention. Thanking is step four. The guy rehashes his sandwich trauma and I furrow my brow, nodding to acknowledge that there's been a problem, even if it's just a mustard-drenched double ham. Lots of times people don't even want anything else—just someone to say they get it, to understand. I'd be more inclined to talk openly about my own sort-of secret if more people were trained in the fine art of customer satisfaction.

"Tessa Masterson, please report to Coffee!" I jerk up when the announcement comes on the loudspeaker. Over at the cash register, Josie gives me a sheepish look. It's not her fault Lucas grabbed the overhead phone from her hands. "Tessa Masterson, emergency in the caffeine aisle." He goes so far as to start singing a Miss Kaboom song, that one on radio repeat all this year: "Shake it like you know what you're made of,' shake it and you'll see what you're afraid of . . ."

I shake my head, caught between laughter and anger. If my parents see me horsing around at work I'm doomed. I hold up my finger for one second to tell Lucas to cool it with the coffee craziness, and then I finish the final step: record. You always want a record of everything, even if it's just the slightest grievance. That way you can prove what happened, have a file on the discord and the solution, so that you and anyone who wants to can see what really happened.

— — — — — —

Outside, the late-afternoon light slants at an odd angle, glinting off the parked delivery trucks out back. Lucas holds the Employee Only door open for me and I notice how the sun lights up the red-gold hairs on his arm. When we were little, he was as smooth as the stones we chucked at each other in the river in back of his apartment house. He'd try to dunk me and I'd wriggle away, collapsing on the riverbank in my wet shorts and T-shirt. He'd be shirt-less in his red swimsuit but I never liked wearing the bikinis everyone else did and my old shorts dried faster in the sun anyway. Summers seemed to last forever back then—just me and Lucas. This was before Giant Brooks became a chain, and we got to raid the one store for cold pop and a hunk of watermelon we took turns balancing on our knees as we rode our bikes back to the shaded swath of trees near the old county farm. We could hide in the tall cornstalks and make our own little world in the rustling green. I didn't know then how much I'd end up hiding later.

"You still on planet Earth, Tessa?" Lucas asks now, still waiting for me to leave the artificial coldness of Giant Brooks and head out to the real world where despite it being only May, the heat radiates off the pavement and instantly makes perspiration appear on my upper lip.

Lucas reaches for my hand and I let my fingers grip his in a quick squeeze as we walk to our usual spot behind one of the delivery platforms.

"I'm here," I tell him but I'm only sort-of here because I want so much to talk to him about what I've been keeping under wraps. Maybe he already knows. I like to think that he knows me well enough to have guessed. That's what's always so funny about newspaper reports or big revelations; most of the time the evidence was there all along. Only most people choose not to see what's right in front of them if it doesn't fit with what they want to be true.

Lucas's brown eyes search mine but I don't know how to explain it without just dropping the big bomb. If he were a customer, I'd know what he wants—maybe my reassurance that this summer will be like all the others. Except it won't—not if I open my usually closed mouth.

"So," he says, and instead of settling into his standard position against the brick wall, he starts to yank me around to the front of the store, which faces our main street. "I have a surprise!"

Lucas's enthusiasm is infectious. He's been able to get me to agree to drop water balloons from the top of the church tower, sneak beers from Giant Brooks to drink tepid on the golf course at midnight, and swim stark naked in the river by his house during the Indian summer we had this past fall. "It's our senior year," he'd said, persuading me with his perfect smile and his crooked eyebrows that hinted at the trouble we might get into in the dark. Everyone used to think Lucas and I had a thing going on but whenever anyone would ask I'd always crack up. So not happening. In Bio in freshman year the first thing we learned was how to collect evidence—how to read the meaning of animal prints in the mud, or sallow skin, or whatever. But since then I've noticed that people don't want to see the evidence, even when you put it right in front of their eyes. My brother, Danny, only asked me that one time and now that he knows the truth, he's never questioned me again.

"I swear you should be in sales," I tell Lucas. "You could make a blind man buy a watch."

Lucas bites his lip, nervous, and wraps his arms around my waist. My stomach clenches. Now I know what he wants but I'm torn in two. One half of me stands here, relishing the familiar feel of his strong hands, the heat, the knowledge that if my parents walked out and caught me taking an extended break when I'm on the clock they'd give me a wink and a mere shake of their heads before taking over my job for me. After all, they are the ones who taught me, trained me for customer service. And Giant Brooks excels at it. Each year for the past decade we've won awards, continued to improve, known how to please the customer. And I know that to make Lucas happy— and probably our parents and his teammates—I'd just have to make myself feel the same way he does.

I look up at Lucas and remember the brief and shining month and a half in seventh grade when I was taller than him. We didn't even slow dance with each other then. It felt too weird, like dancing with myself. Now we dance sometimes but we're both in jeans and sneakers since I hate any shoes that qualify as flats or heels. And I don't dance with his friends because I don't want them to get the wrong idea. So much evidence. But people don't want to use their inner reporter. Don't want to dig. Surface stuff is much easier—for me, too.

Now Lucas takes my face in his hands. "The surprise—" He interrupts himself and puts his lips onto mine.

I pull back, shocked. We hug and lean on each other when we watch movies and stuff but no way have we kissed. In fact, Lucas is one of the reasons I sort of knew. Knew about me not being like every other girl I know: boy crazy. I mean, if I wasn't interested in Lucas that way, who would I like? The guy's gorgeous in that unsure way and makes me laugh and knows how to throw a curveball. And holding hands with him or punching his shoulder or brushing the hair out of his face always felt normal. Close. But right now it's anything but normal. A curveball.

I stammer and blush, which probably makes it look like I'm thrilled but I'm not and I'm sort of stunned that Lucas actually thinks we're taking it—our relationship—a step further. "Wait—"

I back away more than I have to, especially once I notice Josie at the employee door. "Hey," she says, her sandy blond hair covering one eye. I give her a grin. "The eagle has landed." This is our code for my parents coming to check on the store.

I tell Josie, "I'll just be a second." She lingers there a moment more, her eyes questioning mine, before ducking back inside the cool dark hallway. I have to tell him.

Lucas turns my face back toward his. In another universe, Lucas is either a star salesman or a movie star. He's that good-looking, all toned and sprinkled lightly with freckles that play off his red-gold hair. "Aren't you even the slightest bit curious about my surprise?" He takes my backing away from the kiss in stride, as though it were just a question of timing.

"I am, I am," I tell him, but again that little itch inside becomes massive and lets me know I have to pull myself out from the giant cornstalks I've been hiding in. Tell him my own surprise. I glance over my shoulder at the door.

But Lucas isn't waiting for me to talk because even though he knows me, he has his own plan. "First things first," he says, and dashes around the corner and grabs a paper bag. He thrusts it at me, his chest rising from the run and from what I can tell are his nerves.

I reach into the bag and pull out the *Brooks-Mason Beaver*, which is a ridiculous name for a school yearbook and has gone through just about as many jokes as you would expect. "Don't you think it's silly?" I tell him, and I laugh. "I mean, when have we ever had a beaver anywhere remotely close to here?"

Lucas raises his eyebrows as though he sees some cleavage on screen. "Okay . . . How about you put aside the wildlife issues and flip to page one-fifteen." He motions with his hand. When Mrs. Gumble told us to work on our senior pages I thought it would be easy. Pick a quotation, a few lines from that song they played over and over again this fall, the one that sums up senior year, or list some private jokes. But the truth is, senior pages aren't just you summing up who you are. They are summing up what the school needs you to be.

"Remember how you couldn't come up with anything?" he asks, his voice high and excited.

"Of course I remember," I tell him as I hold the closed book against my chest. I tuck a curl back into the messy knot of coils at the back of my head and sigh. "I totally choked. That's why I didn't even order one." It was so unlike me and I couldn't figure out why at first. Then when I talked to Josie about it, I knew. She totally got it. When you're keeping half of yourself under wraps, it's pretty impossible to fill an empty senior page. But that's what I've been feeling this whole year, like a page with no words on it, like a vacant shelf before we stock it. Only what product will be displayed? Real Tessa or the one everyone's been looking at but not really seeing?

"Well, I took care of it!" He grabs the book from me and hurries through the pages to display for me my senior page. Our senior page. Eight-year-old Lucas on his bike, me on mine. He's scanned the photos in to make it look like we're colliding, which we did in real life but no one was there to capture the moment on film. There're no words, just our little-kid selves grinning at each other. "Awesome, right?"

He waits for me to respond. Why didn't he put a more

recent picture? Something about his baseball stats or my track record. Me breaking through the finish line of the marathon last year, the youngest competitor with the fastest time. Or him with his buddy Gus, or Danny, them goofing around on the baseball diamond?

I study the page. "Thanks, Lucas," I tell him, and I mean it even though my voice starts to waver.

"Wait—there's more." He tells me to flip over the paper bag, and on the back of it in green marker he's written RECYCLE ME, so I walk the paper bag over to the big recycling bins underneath the enormous sign that announces sales or Giant Brooks specials for all the world to see.

"Look, Lucas," I say loudly, in the hope that he'll hear me, hear in my voice that I have something to tell him. But my voice gets sucked up into the late-afternoon heat, the distant sound of rushing traffic.

Lucas looks up. I tilt my head, trying to figure out what he sees—a bird? A plane?

Impatient, he puts his hands on my shoulders. "You've got to back up. You can't read it from there." When I'm a few feet away it becomes clear.

TESS + LUCAS = PROM?

It's a simple equation and one that should be true.

In huge electric-blue letters, the kind we keep for megasales.

"I know, I know, maybe you just assumed we'd go

together because, well, I sort of did, too. I mean who else would we go with, right?" Lucas says when I'm turned around and facing him, my mouth hanging open. He's basically blared the question to the entire population of our town.

"It's ecologically sound," I say, trying to inject my voice with a hopefulness I simply don't feel because right now it hits me: if I say yes to Lucas, there's no way I can take someone else. But then—contrary to my ever-present customer-satisfaction skills—I know this, too: just because Lucas wants or assumes I'll go with him, doesn't mean I need to agree. Because the truth is that there is someone else I've pictured dancing with.

"So?" He grins from the side of his mouth, which used to drive me insane when we were little and then made summer girls fall for him. Now it makes me feel sad.

He points up to the twenty-foot-tall illuminated sign. Instead of advertising 85 percent lean chuck on sale, underneath the equation, in case I'm too thick to understand, he's put in block letters:

TESSA MASTERSON, WILL YOU GO TO PROM WITH ME?

I know exactly what he wants and I know the five steps to customer satisfaction, how to give Lucas just the answer he's looking for. Only this time, I can't do it.

4

LUKE

There are tears in her eyes. Once again, the chick flick has educated me well—she's overcome by emotion because I've finally wised up and seen the treasure that was right under my nose the whole time.

She drags a forearm across her face, holds her eyes closed for a few seconds, and then looks at me. And I realize something's wrong because she's not smiling through the tears.

"Lucas," she says. "Oh my God. I'm sorry. I'm sorry, I . . ."

"What? What is it?" I reach out for her arm, and she turns her body away, so I'm reassuringly putting my hand on nothing. My stomach feels like it has imploded—it's a tight little ball of stress and fear. Tessa is crying and won't let me touch her. And every car in Brookfield is driving by and looking at the sign and looking at us. Horns honk.

"About damn time!" somebody yells out.

"Lucas, we need to talk. But not here," she says. She turns and nearly runs through the store to the loading dock. I can feel the eyes of every Giant Brookfield employee burning into me as I run after her.

Most of the big trucks come in late at night, or, more accurately, early in the morning, like when my mom is firing up the bakery ovens, so there's nobody back here. Just me and Tessa and a bunch of wooden pallets and flattened cardboard boxes. There's a nasty, reeking puddle on the concrete floor where somebody dropped a couple dozen eggs and never bothered to clean up. If Tessa's dad finds out who it was, they'll be out of a job tomorrow.

"Lucas," Tessa says, and now she's really crying, tears just rolling down her cheeks. "I thought you knew."

In desperate hope that this whole thing hasn't gone horribly wrong, I fling some chick-flick clichés at her. "That you were—that you and me . . . All along I had the best girl right under my—"

"No!" she shouts. "Crap, this is the problem with not saying stuff. People just fill in the blanks. I love you, Lucas. You're my best friend. But I don't love you like that. I can't. I'm not . . . I mean, God, it's not like I really kept it a secret from you. Every movie we ever watched, I was talking about the female lead. Why do you think I made you watch so many Katharine Hepburn movies?

Why do you think I made you watch *Tank Girl?* Seriously, I really thought you knew."

"Knew what? What the hell are you talking about, T?"

Tessa bites her lip and looks like she might pass out. "That I...I like girls, Lucas. I'm gay. Or lesbian or whatever."

I have nothing to say to that. I plop down on a stack of pallets.

And now Tessa walks over to me and puts a hand on my shoulder. I don't twist away because I'm not like that, but her hand on my shoulder doesn't feel electric the way it has for the past couple of weeks. It just feels heavy and too warm.

"I guess I've always known, really. But it wasn't till Josie and I started...I don't know if you can even call it going out in Brookfield because, you know, we can't really go anywhere besides my basement...." She gives a sad chuckle.

And now I shrug her hand away and spring to my feet. "You've always known? You've *always* known?"

Tessa staggers back a couple of steps. "Well. Yeah. I mean...yeah."

"And you never thought you should tell me."

"Well, like I said, I never talked about guys or anything, and I really thought you had just put two and two together—" Tessa's mouth wrinkles.

"Best friends for most of our lives and this little detail about you wasn't something you thought you should share with me? I've told you about every single girlfriend I've ever had, and you have a . . . God. I don't even want to know. But you start . . . going out with someone, and you don't even see fit to tell me. You have to wait until I make an ass of myself in front of the whole town!"

"I just can't do it," she says, and the tears are back. "I mean, I could have done it, we could have gone as friends and had everyone assume I'm something I'm not, but I'm almost eighteen, you know? I'm an adult! I can't pretend to be something I'm not anymore!"

"Like my friend?" I say.

"No, Lucas, of course—"

"Because friends tell each other stuff like this! That's what you don't even get! I have never . . . God, I feel so stupid right now. I've shared like every single thing I've ever thought with you, and you had . . . your whole self . . . excuse me. I'm upset, and I have to go take down a big lighted sign in front of the whole town!"

I storm out of the loading dock. Tessa doesn't run after me. I head over to the utility closet and grab the big fifteen-foot-long claw we use to change the letters on the sign. It's heavy and awkward, and the tears that I'm trying to hold back are making my vision blurry. Fortunately, I can cut through the parking lot so I don't have to walk through the store with a big claw. Which is good because I'd probably knock a whole bunch of stuff down. Possibly even accidentally.

So I trudge through the parking lot, set up the ladder,

and make the really long climb up to the sign. I left the box of plastic letters out here when I set this up a million years ago. Or an hour ago. Whichever it was.

I start at the end, pulling off the plastic letters and dumping them into the box. Question mark. Into the box. That question's been answered. ME. Into the box. WITH. PROM.

I wish I could say I was so intent on my humiliating task that I was able to shut out everything around me, but I hear every honk, every call of "Loser!" and every single person who comes out of the store and says something like "Luke? Are you okay? What happened?"

They don't really care. They just want the gossip. And this gossip is certainly going to be hot. The news of my big, failed sign-gesture is going to spread through all of Indiana. I can pretty much guarantee that when I take the mound against Campbell County Regional next Tuesday, their fans will be singsong chanting "Tessss-a! Tessss-a!" at me. Awesome.

The sign comes down and I put back the more useful, but probably less interesting news that pork round is on sale this week.

5

Tessa

What about this one?" Danny asks, holding up a light-blue suit with overly wide lapels. "I think I can pull it off."

If anyone could wear outdated bell-bottomed Prom gear leftover from when Journey first sang "Don't Stop Believin'" and Miss Kaboom wasn't even born, it would be my brother. I give him a grin but shake my head as I sink onto the vinyl bench by the rental shoes. "I'm not sure Anabel would be psyched about that."

Danny and I are what my grandmother used to call Irish twins, born nine months apart, and since he's abnormally smart he's in my grade. He's also abnormally tall, which makes people assume he's older than I am. I sigh, watching him navigate the store. Mr. Tux is off Route 90 in a faded strip mall that I'm sure will be snatched up by a big chain store soon but that for now has only a shuttered Thai takeout place, a bowling alley known mainly for its underage drinking and conveniently located next to the Discount LiquorMart, and Mr. Tux, where all the guys rent their gear for weddings, the Fall Formal, and the Prom. Everyone, that is, who is going.

"I still don't get why you're not shopping with Anabel," Danny says as though he can read my mind. We're eerily twin-like in that way. Danny knows about me. Has known for pretty much ever, even though I never really had to say anything to him after that first time. I wish the rest of the world were like that.

"It's weird enough how much time we all spend together," I tell him, and point to a plain black tux on a rack in the corner. Danny investigates it but then shrugs it off. Probably not cool enough for him; he likes to stand out. Or, as he puts it, would prefer not to look like every other hick who slapped on a Mr. Tux discount special (coupon in the weekly town paper) before rocking out at the Embassy Suites faux waterfall post-Prom. "Besides, it's not like my style really meshes with Anabel's."

Danny's girlfriend, Anabel, is of the school that anything tight and short can always be made tighter and shorter. I fully expect her to show up in the rental limo looking glamorous and way older than eighteen, whereas the few times I've been made to wear a dress I've felt horrible in my skin.

"You know I'm not a heels-and-satin kind of person." I give him *the look*, which he registers right away.

"So don't wear the heels. Be creative," he says as though it's no big deal. As if not every girl in Brookfield-Mason Regional High pays to get her hair coiffed and slithers herself into some gown she'll never wear again. When I was a bridesmaid at my cousin's wedding I had to wear this purple strappy number. Instead of feeling like the most beautiful version of myself, I felt like I was trapped in a costume that made me invisible. I looked at the grooms-men not because they were cute—they were, not even close to being my type—but because their tuxes looked good. Straightforward. Honest. Comfortable.

"Just what is your style these days?" Danny asks, sit-ting next to me as he wriggles his foot in its dirty athletic sock into a shiny black dress shoe that looks comical with his baseball pants and Brookfield Regional green T-shirt. My stomach turns as I think about Lucas in that same out-fit at practice today, his pitching arm warm in the jacket he slings on, his eyes steely and intense. We've success-fully avoided each other today but we'll be face-to-face at our adviser meeting. The hurt tugs at my chest when I think of wounding him, but I reassure myself that he'll understand; he'll cool off and support me, right?

I read online once (and later erased evidence of my search) about this girl in California who told her whole softball team about being a lesbian because she was totally in love with the catcher. And falling in love is a good reason to come out. And it's true that I like Josie. A lot. But she's not why I felt the words about to burst from my mouth when he asked me. It's Lucas. He's who I told when my parents thought they'd go bankrupt back when gas prices soared and they didn't know if they'd get the loan for the Giant Brooks expansion. He's who I told first about wanting to be premed even though most kids from our town don't even go to college, except maybe a two-year community college or beautician school. He's the one who listened to me cry when my grandma couldn't remember who I was anymore. She couldn't even remember who *she* was anymore, and how sad is that, forgetting your own self? And Lucas, well, he believed in me and did this thing where he'd squeeze each of my fingertips until I wasn't scared or sad or pissed off.

So he's why. Lucas needed to know the truth, and I had to be the one to tell him. Somehow, telling Lucas is like admitting that it's real. That *it*—the liking girls— isn't going to evaporate.

Danny nudges me and frowns. "I was just kidding, Tess. No big deal."

Except it is a big deal. "Um, Danny?" He looks distracted as he fiddles with the too-short laces. "I sort of have a style."

"I know, I know, I'm just a dumb jock who knows nothing about fashion."

"You only say things like that because you're not a dumb jock and everyone knows it." He's going to MIT in the fall, ditching baseball and the entire Midwest for robotic engineering.

I smooth my hair in the back and pull my black tank top down over my hips, flapping my flip-flops out of nervousness. "No. What I mean is, this is sort of it." I point to my plain top and under-the-radar jeans. "Everyone overlooks all the signs, but here's the sign. Me. Not dating boys. Me, in jeans and a tank top. It's sort of who I am."

Danny keeps struggling with his shoes, not ignoring me exactly but not paying much attention either. "It's not all of who you are," he mumbles.

"That's true . . . but I can't help feeling that everyone else is sort of summed up by their outfits. Take Anabel . . ." Danny raises his eyebrows. "You kind of knew about her before you knew her, right? Tight dresses . . . not that I'm a fan of judging anyone by their cover . . ."

"But sure, yeah. And you can tell I'm the awesome athletic stud by my jacket, I guess."

"Or Gus, how he wears John Deere T-shirts every chance he gets."

"Farmer's kid," Danny says of his best friend.

"So here I am displaying my . . . lack of . . ."

"Wanting to date males?" Danny offers.

I give him a wry grin. "But no one picks up on the signs. Never dated a guy. Never wears skirts. You'd think people would put two and two together."

"You know what they say, 'Don't ask, don't tell.'" Danny mimes a soldier salute.

I stand up and lean for a minute on the glass counter that houses the accessories. There, amid the silver-plated and overly shiny gold button covers, is a pair of cuff links. "These," I say, "are cool. Yin and yang. See? This outer circle represents 'everything,' while the black and white shapes inside are an interaction of two energies . . ." Danny saunters over to see what I'm pointing to. He leans his tan forearm on the counter. "Yin is white and yang is black but each has a bit of the other in it." I look at Danny. I bite my lip, thinking. "Just like things in life aren't totally black or white, one can't exist without the other. Maybe I need a bigger sign." I think of the enormity of Lucas's sign out front of the store, the empty spaces where his question used to be. How now it's covered in mismatching letters spelling "pork round."

"Huh?" Danny wrinkles his forehead. "I'm going with the rocker look, with this jacket." He grabs a midnight-blue shiny number from the rack and holds it up to his chest. "No tie. Open dress shirt with something cool underneath." He loves to joke, and holds out a complete tuxedo, black pants and matching jacket, a slightly ruffled shirt underneath. "You can have this one."

I pause, letting the idea form in my head. "You know, I think you're on to something." Yes, Danny "knows," and I thought Lucas might have, though clearly he didn't, but why should the people in my life have to be split into groups who know and groups who don't? Can't it be ask and tell? How can I keep it straight—ha-ha—between people who see the me as a fraud and those who see the real me? And liking girls is only one part of me. I know that. But it is a part. I picture Danny and Lucas ready for Prom night and ready for their girls. Lucas is his friend, his teammate, and the guy who is meant to split the cost of the limo on Prom night.

Danny holds the tuxedo on one finger, confused, looking out of place in his baseball uniform and dress shoes. "Lucas nearly took my head off with his curveball today. So you guys aren't going to Prom together, that much is clear. What, he didn't want to be your fake date?"

I take the tuxedo from him and hold it to me like it offers protection. "No. He wanted to be my real date. Somehow I thought Lucas of all people would know." I study the suit. "But I have an idea."

"You never told him?" Danny asks. I shake my head. Danny sighs. "There's more?"

I nod. "I think I actually want to go to the Prom," I say, and it feels like I'm admitting something.

Danny smiles. "I knew it. You so want to wear panty hose."

"I so do not." I swat at him and he flinches. "I just think I want to go with Josie."

Quiet stretches out so long I think I'll melt right into the tacky linoleum floor. The salesperson coughs so I pretend to be talking about Prom things, gesturing with the tuxedo.

"Josie B.?" Danny asks as though the name can't possibly be right.

"Yeah." I nod as I find a slim tie and hand it to him.

"The deli girl?" Danny's face is caught between confusion and congratulations.

"You're always telling me to find 'the right person,'" I remind him, and my heart chugs along waiting for him to get exactly what I mean.

"And the one who gives out free slices of Genoa salami to the annoying toddlers is the right one?"

"Truth?" I ask, and my brother nods. Relief. "I don't know. I mean, I guess she is—for now, anyway. I like her. Yeah." I smile. "But more than that, it's like I'm ready to stop . . ."

"Hiding?"

I take a huge breath like I'm about to go way deep down under water. "Yes." I force my eyes to meet my brother's.

He stands there, his mouth open until he realizes how it looks. "No wonder Lucas seemed like he was ready to set things on fire today. You let him go through the trouble of the big Prom gesture—"

"Is it my fault Lucas always does things over-the-top? I didn't tell him to ask me like that!" I will the tears in my eyes to stay put.

"But you didn't tell him not to, either." Danny looks personally offended on behalf of all guys.

"Nothing much, you know, has happened . . . with

Josie, I mean." My voice feels small and the words sink into the clothing around us.

Danny's face brightens. "Oh—well, that's something to look forward to . . . big Prom night!" He pauses. I give him a fast nod, waiting to see where he's going with all of this. "So it's not that you don't want to go to the Prom the way we planned . . . it's more like you need to rearrange the equation?"

I smile. "I knew you'd get it." Danny gives a wary smile back. "That's right. That's what I'm trying to say. I want everything to be like it was. Only with—"

"Just with, um, a girl. The deli girl."

"Don't call her that, Dan. And don't wear your baseball pants on Prom night." I make him laugh but then his face crumples, as it always does when he's sorting something out. "What?"

"Are you still gonna rent the limo with us—I mean, with me?"

I shrug. "I hope so." It means a lot that he still wants to, so I give him the sibling stare back and he gets it without me having to say so.

Danny looks serious. "It's just . . . I'm not sure how Anabel's going to feel about it, you know? She sort of had that double-date thing in her mind. The shared suite at the hotel and all." Danny raises his eyebrows so I'll get his point.

"Oh. Oh!" I say, cluing in. We stand there with the rental clothing until the idea finishes forming in my mind.

How humiliating it would have been to be in some floral-bedspreaded hotel room while Danny and Anabel romanced the hours away on one of the beds and me and Lucas ... what, played cards or stole tiny shampoos from the utility cart. "I have an idea. About the hiding, I mean. And my style ... this!"

I hold up the tuxedo. It is perfectly black, new, with the tags on, and the shirt ruffled just enough to have that feminine edge. "If I sucked it up and wore black heels? And my hair up?" I try to demonstrate and Danny doesn't know whether to burst out laughing or yell for help. "No, really! See? I'll still be the double date, only with Josie. And you'll be the rock star smart jock with your hot Glama-bel." I can picture it: the warm night air, the slim-cut tuxedo, corsages.

Danny breaks my reverie. "And just where is Lucas in this scenario? I mean, don't get me wrong. I'm your brother and I'll, you know, accept whatever curveball you throw my way—"

"Ohh, warning, sports analogy!" I say, and we both grin but Danny goes right back into his speech.

"But not everyone's like that." He shakes his hair into his eyes. Like mine, it's the color of an old penny, only his isn't as wildly curly as mine. He looks at me through his fringe. "And Lucas—he's ... I don't know how he's going to take all this."

I bite my top lip and look at myself in the full-length mirror. The tux is too long, but it could be hemmed. And

I have some money saved from extra shifts at my Giant Brooks job. "But he didn't say anything about it today?" I press the tux against my chest, imagining dancing in it. I know that the tux is just a superficial thing, but it feels like so much more. Like if I wear it to the Brookfield-Mason Prom I'll be announcing myself. The real Tessa Masterson. And everyone will finally know. I'll feel the relief you only feel when you have nothing to hide.

Danny shrugs. "Actually Lucas didn't say anything. So maybe that's a good sign. Sometimes at games when he gets pissed off he swallows it so he doesn't go nuts. Then he cools down."

"Maybe that's what he's doing," I say, and hope makes my voice a bit louder. I look at the tux in the mirror and see my brother looking at me too. "You gotta admit—it's going to look good." Josie showed me a photo strip of her and her old girlfriend from a fair at her last school right after the girlfriend had told everyone. They both looked so happy. And when I studied the pictures, I was jealous. Not just because of the old-girlfriend part of the story. But because of the relief I knew they must have felt. The relief Josie carries with her every day.

"You're kind of wacky, you know that?" Danny puts his hand on my shoulder like he might pull me back from an edge of some kind, but then knows he doesn't need to. "But I totally think you can rock a tux."

Danny grins and we fling our items onto the counter while the salesperson raises her eyebrows at my purchase.

I hand over my cash card and look out the window where even the deserted strip mall is sunny. I remember playing touch football with Lucas and how he always thought I looked good in his freshman football jersey. Maybe he's already getting used to this, just like I am. And things won't be as bad as I think.

6

LUKE

LUKE FOGELMAN, WILL YOU GO TO PROM WITH ME?

These words are written in marker in a speech balloon coming out of the mouth of a photo of Miss Piggy that is taped to my locker. Not sure if Miss Piggy's face is a reference to the pork round that's still on sale at Giant Brooks or what.

I grab the paper, crumpling it and tearing it off my locker at the same time. I don't throw it on the ground because I was raised better than that. I actually walk eight extra steps past a trash can to get it into a recycling bin.

When I get back to my locker, Patrick Schmidt is standing there.

"Dude," he says as I spin my lock, "what happened?"

"Don't really want to talk about it," I say, dumping

textbooks and binders into my bag. I close my locker, spin the lock, and head down the hall.

"Shot down!" Pat says. I know this is what guys do. Another thing that guys do is punch somebody who disrespects them in the face, but I decide that rejected *and* suspended would make for a pretty crappy week. So I just give him the finger as I walk away.

Normally this is the part where I would go talk to Tessa about how crappy I feel, but since she's the reason I'm feeling crappy and she's a liar who can't be trusted, I'm not going to do that.

My phone buzzes.

"You still not talking to me?" reads the text from Tessa. I don't answer it, which is my answer. She's called me a few times and left voice mails, but I am not talking to her. This is partly just out of revenge—she made me look stupid, so I'm pissed—but it's also that I don't know what to say to her. I feel like our whole friendship was a lie. She's probably the only person I've ever really opened up to, and the whole time she was hiding stuff from me. I just don't feel like I can trust somebody like that.

I head into the bathroom. I don't know if the same marker-wielding genius is responsible for the obscene graffiti over the urinal that begins TESSA MASTERSON, WILL YOU . . . or if the whole town just had a meeting and decided to taunt me in the same way today.

The whole day, I hear people snickering at me. Of course I know the word "laughingstock." It was in our eighth-grade vocabulary book. But I don't think I ever really fully understood it until today.

— — — — —

Mom has Tuesday off, so she's waiting for me when I get home from practice at six. "Come on, kid," she says. "Road trip."

I throw my sweat-soaked, salt-encrusted hat on the table. "Mom, I just want to—"

Mom picks the hat up with two fingers, holding it at the very edge of the brim. "Okay. Take a shower first. You smell. And then we're taking a road trip."

"Mom. I don't feel like—"

"Sorry—I don't really remember asking you. Did I ask you? Oh, that's right. I told you. This is my weekend and I'm gonna enjoy it with my favorite person in Brookfield. Only we have to get the hell out of Brookfield to enjoy it."

I try really hard to stay sullen enough to have a fight with Mom, but she disarms me with the "favorite person" line. Plus, as anyone at Giant Brookfield can tell you, nobody wins an argument with my mom.

So I hop in the shower and a few minutes later we hop into our pathetic little Ford Focus and start driving.

"Mom, I can't really go all the way to Cincinnati. I've got school in the morning and—"

"Relax, Nancy. We're not going all the way to Cincinnati."

Mom, who has an affection for Miss Kaboom that is totally ridiculous for a woman her age, makes us listen to the entire *Space Party* album on the way.

"Mom, this is fourteen-year-old-girl music."

"It's not either. It's dance music that anyone can enjoy. And I love Miss Kaboom. She's just—she lets her freak flag fly, you know? She does her thing and doesn't give a shit what anybody thinks. Tell me you don't admire that!"

"I mean, when you put it that way, yeah, but I wish she was expressing that idea in better music."

"We'll listen to your music on the way back, okay?"

"Fine."

Miss Kaboom is just finishing telling us she's fine the way she is as we pull up into the parking lot of the LA Star Casino in Hidden Valley, Indiana.

"Mom, I'm too young to gamble."

"And I'm too sensible. We're going to have dinner and laugh at the casino patrons and the Elvis impersonator."

"Elvis impersonator? Seriously? This is supposed to cheer me up?"

"Wait'll you see him. He's definitely late-period Elvis. He'll make you glad to be eighteen and athletic at least."

We sit down in the Brown Derby Lounge, which is on the roof of the LA Star Casino, a floating "stationary boat" that sits on the surface of Hidden Valley Lake. It's a nice cool night and not too buggy, which is pretty amazing. We get burgers and fries, and I'm halfway through my food and feeling a little relaxed when Mom finally gets into it.

"So you wanna tell me what happened?" she says, all fake casual while she puts more ketchup on her fries.

"Actually, if I wanted to tell you, I would have," I say.

"Okay. Don't want to. But do it anyway. You're kind of crappy company when you're all sulky, so you might as well spill the beans."

I stare at my fries. "It's embarrassing," I say.

"I wiped poo off your butt for the first two years of your life. It is totally impossible for you to be embarrassed in front of me." This line is delivered just as our waitress, Denise, who has perfect teeth, long brown hair pulled back into a ponytail, and a rack that's straining at the boundaries of her Brown Derby Lounge uniform polo shirt, returns to our table to ask us if everything is okay.

"Except for my mom talking about poo, everything's fine," I tell Denise. Mom shrugs, her mouth full of burger, and Denise looks at me like I am the weirdest person in the entire tri-state area. I guess I should be used to that by now, but I'm not.

Denise walks away, and though she's a small-minded idiot who doesn't appreciate a good poo joke, she does have a fantastic butt that I can't help staring at.

"Don't do that. It makes me uncomfortable," Mom says. "She's not an object. She's an idiot, but she still deserves some respect."

"Yeah, well, I tried being friends with a girl, and that

didn't exactly work out," I say. Damn it. Mom tricked me again. Or maybe I really did want to talk about it.

"So that's it?" Mom says. "Years of friendship down the tubes because she didn't want to go to Prom with you?"

"It's not just that," I say.

"I mean, that's got to be pretty embarrassing, the thing with the sign," Mom continues.

"Do you think?" I bark back at her.

"Yeah," she says. "I do. And I'm really, really sorry."

On the other end of the roof, guys are banging drums and tuning guitars. A guy in a Brown Derby Lounge apron walks to the mic and says, "Ladies and gentlemen, LA Star Casino is proud to present Ron Ferguson as Elvis!"

The band springs into action and a guy in his late fifties, gut about ready to explode out of his rhinestone-spangled white jumpsuit, strolls to the middle of the cramped stage. "Thank you very much," he says, and a couple of ladies in their sixties next to the stage actually scream.

"Mom, if the old ladies start throwing their underwear at him, I am going to vomit and leave, in that order."

"And I'll be right behind you. So what's Tessa's problem? Why doesn't she want to go to Prom with the best-looking guy in Brookfield?"

"Okay, that makes me uncomfortable. I owe you at least one remark about Denise's fantastic rack for that."

"That counts. As a remark about her breasts."

"No, it doesn't. That was just a remark about a remark."

"Whatever. So what's Tessa's excuse?"

"This one's called 'Polk Salad Annie,'" Ron Ferguson exclaims.

"She's . . . she's . . . uh, not romantically interested in me."

Mom stares at me for long seconds. Ron Ferguson gyrates. Old ladies sigh.

"Why the hell not? It's not like she's got another boyfriend, is it?"

"No. Not a boyfriend. No. Not a *boy*friend."

"You mean she's—"

"Yep." I stare intently at my plate. Everything's going cold, and it's all a lot less appealing than it was before.

"Oh, the poor kid. Her poor parents. And her hair's so long, too. I never would have guessed it."

"The poor—her poor—Mom, what about me? What about poor me?"

Mom looks at me. "You've had your heart broken. And except for having me as a mom, you're exactly what Brookfield wants everybody from Brookfield to be. But Tessa's not. She never will be. The Mastersons took a fair amount of grief for hiring a single mother in disgrace seventeen years ago. How do you think the good folks at First Lutheran and the purity-ring people are going to react when they find out Tessa's . . . like that?"

"Who cares?" I take a bite of food.

"I care. And you should, too. If she's your friend."

"She's not my friend, or she would have told me who she really was before I made a total idiot of myself in front of the whole town."

"Yeah, you're a guy who makes grand romantic gestures. What an idiot. What girl would want a guy like that?"

"Thank you very much," Ron Ferguson says. "We're gonna take it down a little bit with a song from *Blue Hawaii*. This is 'Can't Help Falling in Love.'"

Ron Ferguson starts crooning about how he can't help falling in love, and stupid Ron Ferguson in his stupid white jumpsuit pretending to be someone he's not makes me start to cry. "I gotta go," I say. "I'll meet you in the car." I stand up and leave to go sit in the Ford Focus. Mom arrives half an hour later.

"One of the old ladies honest-to-God threw her panties at him," Mom says. I don't say anything, and we drive home.

——— ——— ——— ——— ——— ———

Work at Giant Brooks is way easier than school. A lot of people at work are older and so don't feel the need to kick me when I'm down the way other teenagers do. Either that or my mom has put the word out that anybody who messes with me in my current state will be looking at the business end of a rolling pin.

Either way, work is pretty bearable. Especially because Tessa's not there.

I'm taking my fifteen in the break room when Kate Sweeney comes walking in. I used to bag at her register last year before she went to college. I kind of thought Tessa was jealous, but maybe it was because of the attention

Kate was paying to me instead of the other way around. "Hey," she says.

"Hey," I say. "I thought you escaped Brookfield forever."

"I'm just back for the summer. The Mastersons gave me a few shifts a week, mostly just so I don't get bored to death."

"Well. Welcome back. Not much has changed since you left."

Kate puts seventy-five cents into the vending machine and watches as the wire in slot A4 spins but does not release her bag of Baked Lay's. She bangs on the side, grits her teeth, and puts a dollar in. The machine spits out a quarter and two bags of Baked Lay's.

"Want one of these?" she says.

"Nah, I've got some cardboard boxes out back I like to chew on. More flavorful."

Kate smiles. "Suit yourself." She rips open a bag. "So you're big news around here."

"Yeah," I say. I hope my tone of voice communicates this: "I don't currently hate you, but I will if this conversation continues."

Apparently it does. "Well, I think that was really sweet," she says, walking out of the break room. "Enjoy your cardboard."

"You enjoy yours," I say.

— — — — — —

Unfortunately, I can't spend all my time at work, and I have to go back to school. The graffiti bandit has stopped posting new parodies of my sign, but people still want to talk to me and make jokes and stuff, and it's tiresome.

A couple of people tell me Tessa was at the tux store in Mason with Danny—who, like all my teammates, is getting the silent treatment from me—and that she rented a tux. I feel like this is one of those typical Brookfield stories where something essential is missing and everyone loses their shit until they find out the story was totally wrong. So I pretty much ignore it. I mean, she wouldn't be dumb enough to do something like that. Would she?

7

⋈

Tessa

Our kitchen looks like we're either massive food hoarders or are preparing a hideout, a fallout shelter from some war outside. Giant Brookfield dumps all the extras with us—cans with misprinted labels, flats of Cola Light about to expire even though there's nothing in the ingredient list that could possibly expire, and heaps of potato chips, pretzels, and cheese puffs. Different brands send bulk packages to inspire Mom and Dad to order cases for the stores. Most of the time they stick with what they know and order your standard salted and BBQ chips. Every once in a while they throw caution to the wind and order something super-exotic like artificial, not-in-any-way-European French Onion.

"Now tell me these are worth the extra nineteen cents

per packet," my dad says to my mom, rustling a blue-and-gold bag of Bestler's Biggest Cheddar 'n' Onion Super-Size Cheezers.

My mom looks skeptical. "I'll try one if you will, Tess." She slips her slim hand in and takes two oversize chips out, handing one to me, seemingly oblivious to my nerves and my racing heart. "Well?"

I force myself to crunch and chew halfway through the mildly disgusting snack despite my dry mouth, my sweaty palms. My mother's mouth is dusted with cheese. Before she notices any awkwardness, I make my move.

"Probably you're wondering where my magical Prom dress is," I say, trying to anticipate a problem the way she and my dad taught me. Dad sits at the round kitchen table doing his best to consume the rest of the contents of the Super-Size Cheezers bag; he and my mom are often so busy at the markets that they forget to eat and then come home and make weird dinners from whatever snacks and wheels of cheese have been dropped off on the front porch.

My mom dusts off her lips with one of the paper napkins that come in packs of five hundred and that we keep on the counter.

"Well, where is it?" Dad asks when Mom doesn't.

I pause, wondering how on earth to explain. These are people who blanch at new snack products. How will they handle this news about their daughter? My cheeks flush and I feel woozy.

"Now listen," Mom says as she stands up. She puts a

hand on my forehead as though checking for a fever. "I might be a million years old but I still remember the pre-Prom jitters." Air gets caught in my throat as I try to breathe. My mom looks at me and then over her shoulder at my dad and his bright orange fingers, his mustache partly dyed by fake cheese. "Listen . . . your Dad and I . . . Well . . ."

This is it, I think. They know. They know. And they're not freaking out. I always worry about things exploding and they rarely do. The tiniest of smiles appears on my lips.

"So." I sigh. "You understand?"

My dad studies a new juice bottle, some combination of iced tea and lemonade with a cartoon lime on the label. "I was the first to say maybe things with Luke would progress to the next level."

My forehead wrinkles. "What?"

My mom steps in. "What he means is, you two spend an awful lot of time together as it is and maybe you have your doubts or feel certain pressures from Lucas because he's a teenage boy." She says "boy" like it means "sex," and I cringe. "So I completely understand where you're coming from in terms of wanting to forget going to the Prom with him." She pats my back like it's all settled. "But . . ." She and my dad do another parental check-in, with only their eyes communicating.

"We think you'd regret not going at all. That's how come we told your brother to make sure you got something today." My dad stands up. "Don't get that look, Tessa." He motions to my face. "We'll even reimburse you for what you spent." I can see dollar signs behind my dad's eyes. He's not big on buying stuff for us, always wants us to make our own money so we appreciate the value of the hard-earned American dollar, so it's an even bigger deal that he and Mom want to fund my Prom gear.

"But Dad—"

"Dad's right, honey. You said no to Lucas but that doesn't mean you can't still enjoy yourself!" My mother is perpetually bright. Glass half full, sunny side of the street. The early-evening light touches the counter, the breeze riffles the sunflower-yellow curtains my mom sewed by hand when I was little. Being in this room has always felt like being in the center of a flower, that sunny and happy.

I dash out of the kitchen to the mudroom where I dropped my book bag and hung up the plastic suit bag from Mr. Tux. Another life lesson I've learned from customer service is accountability, so I don't want to blame anything on Lucas. After all, he's always been there for me. Well, not the past day or so, but probably that'll pass. I hold the suit bag with two fingers, fully aware that its contents are not what my parents expect.

"Now," I say, when I get back into the kitchen, "let me just start by saying this might be a big sur—"

Dad shakes his head and slams his palms on the tabletop. "What did I tell you, Louise? She's gone and bought something obscene." He looks at me with his bushy eyebrows raised. "Let me guess—it's up to here?" He marks a point at the top of his thigh.

"Strapless?" my mother offers, reaching for the bag, determined to find out for herself.

Weirdly, I wish Lucas were here. Well, not present-day pissed-off Lucas, not public Prom-asking Lucas, but friend Lucas. Old Lucas. The one who'd help me. Who would hold my hand in a friendly, supportive way.

"Well?" my protective father booms.

"It's not short," is how I start. And I open my mouth, intending to pour the whole story out, to explain that it's not Lucas. It's not them. It's not anything sudden, it's more like a creeping knowledge that I've pushed away for as long as I can remember. Until Lucas asked me to Prom I thought I could just keep shoving that part of me away until—when? College? After college? When is the right time? Never. Now. And there's Josie and the artful playlists she burns on CDs and decorates with permanent markers. And how fun it would be to dance with her to some of those songs. The Pogues or the Pixies or Miss Kaboom belting out "Shake it, shake it." I've gone so far as to imagine the corsages we'd get each other. But I also know that it's not just Josie. If it weren't her, it'd be someone else. Some other girl some other time. I chomp on my upper lip until it hurts. "In fact, the dress is, well, it's not even—"

Right when I'm about to let the tux out of the bag, our obnoxious old-school rotary phone rings, shocking the kitchen quiet. Even the happy curtains seem shocked. My mother answers with a quick "yup," the way she always does, continuing to mull over the suit bag, which is, thankfully, out of her reach. My dad rummages around for the main course—from the looks of it, a tray of deli meat made into fancy rolls and garnished with now-wilting parsley someone ordered, paid for with at least a 50 percent deposit, and then probably forgot to pick up. As he wolfs down a turkey-and-provolone roll-up, my mother says, "I see," into the phone, but twists her lips in confusion. She hangs up before I can reconsider and slink out toward the living room to try Lucas's cell phone yet again.

The receiver clatters into the yellow base on the wall. "That was Melinda Driscoll. She's down at the former Thai Palace—she's the real estate agent there," my mother says, her voice hard and flat. "She seems to be under the impression that, for some reason, you bought—not rented, but purchased—a tuxedo today."

I swallow. Thai Palace, now closed, is next to the Discount LiquorMart, which is a couple of stores down from Mr. Tux. Word wouldn't have to travel far from there to be spewed from Mrs. Driscoll's big mouth. I keep poised, fully in my customer-service stance. "Well, the thing is, it was on sale, so—"

"And Danny managed to convince you to pay for it? I said I'd cover your dress, not his outfit. He's in for a grounding." My father's voice reverberates against the lemony walls.

Danny has a tendency to make rash decisions, especially involving money or fun things that my parents perceive of as flights of fancy and unnecessary. Exhibit A: the pinball machine in the basement. Exhibit B: his water bed. "No," I say, defending Danny. "This isn't Danny's fault."

My mother takes this opportunity to snatch the bag from my arms where it has left a trail of perspiration. Swiftly she unzips it and looks inside. "What a foolish boy," she says. "It says FINAL SALE *and* it's ridiculously small."

"Maybe he's planning on hacking an inch or two off his legs?" my dad jokes.

"But that's the thing. It's not for Danny." The words hang there and I watch my parents sort through the possibilities: it's for Lucas, but no, because he's not going with Tessa, or it's for . . . "It's for me."

My dad stops snarfing salty processed meats. My mother adjusts her practical khakis and fitted blouse as though just now realizing what she's wearing.

After what feels like hours my mother finally asks, "Is this a joke?"

The expression on her face is the same one she had when the original Giant Brookfield, the one closest to her heart, was robbed. They broke the front plate-glass window and looted the cash registers and damaged the expensive display cases, unplugging them and ruining the food inside.

"I'm sure there's a reasonable explanation for all of this," my dad says, ever the practical person. "Right?" His gaze locks on mine.

I shift in my sneakers. "Um, well, yeah. The explanation is very simple. I saw the tux at the store and it looked . . . great. Like it would really *fit* me. Me, you know? Like finally I wouldn't shove myself into a dress just so everyone else was happy."

"Is this to do with Lucas?" My mother struggles to understand, which, instead of making me feel angry at her, only makes me feel worse.

"Look," I say to her, and take the tux back. I slide it out from its sheath and hold it up to me. "See? It's not Lucas. It's not Danny. It's not school pressure or any of those things you're probably thinking." I go back to the customer-service tactics. "I understand you must be shocked."

"Don't try those customer-service techniques with us!" my dad shouts. "Two seconds ago I had a daughter who I thought was going to dress like a hooker for her Prom. That seems like a manageable problem now."

"Dad—you still have a daughter." I try to smile. "And I'd never dress like a hooker."

My mom reasons, planning in her head. "I saw the cover of *Us Weekly*. This is popular in Hollywood? For girls to wear boys' clothing?" Her voice goes up, her hopes go higher.

I shrug. "You know I'm not the biggest gossip-rag reader. The cashiers know more than I do." I keep the tux pressed to my body, already imagining my hair up in a twist.

My dad looks relieved. "So we can tell Mrs. Driscoll this is a fad? A trend?"

I shake my head. "No. I'm pretty sure I'll be the only female at the Prom in a tux." Their faces aren't crumpling so I move forward. "And there's something else—"

The screen door slams and Danny bursts into the house, shouting information while dropping his baseball bat and gear onto the floor in his usual messy heap. "Word's out, Tess! Just so you know, the whole team somehow found out about it. Didn't take long—like an hour, right? And now you and your big old Prom date are the talk of the town."

"Date?" My mother braces herself on the table's edge.

"Mom and Dad are here!" I shout even though it's too late, and Danny keeps blathering on about every detail. I mean, I haven't even asked Josie yet. Yet. Of course I want to. I spent last night flipping my pillow around to the cool side every half hour trying to figure out if she'd say yes or if it was dumb to ask her to this traditional event. Now it looks like I won't even get a chance.

"Lucas is taking it rough, man. I mean, like rough and ragged." Danny walks into the kitchen, grabs one of the lemonade teas and swigs most of it in one gulp while my parents watch in amazement at everything.

"Define rough," I say, my lungs cramping, my feet tingling.

"Like the kind of pissed off that might make him do something stupid," Danny says, sweat dripping from his sideburns to his jaw.

I feel instant betrayal even though I don't know what—if anything—Lucas is doing. "Well, maybe like you said he just needs to cool down."

"Wait—can we backtrack a second here?" My father's big frame takes up nearly the whole window, blocking the last of the sunlight and darkening the room.

Danny elbows me. "Didn't you tell them?"

I cut to the chase. "Fine. First I thought I didn't want to go to the Prom. Like it was kind of gratuitous spending like you said when we wanted that arcade game at the front of the store."

"I still love Ms. Pac-Man," Danny says. "She's hot . . . in a cartoony way."

I poke his arm. "Not helping . . . But then I realized it was all this pressure, this immense weight on my shoulders about finding some shiny dress and renting a long black car and a hotel room—"

"Hotel room?" my father yells.

"Suite, Dad, a suite," Danny interjects with his usual intentional sarcasm.

"No friggin' way!" Dad's bellow is loud enough to reach two counties over.

I roll my eyes. "Well, you can be glad that that's not happening, Dad. It felt wrong. I felt like I was lying. Not just to Lucas. To everyone. To myself."

My mother's voice comes out small, nearly a whisper. "May I ask you something?" I nod. "This tux you're planning on wearing . . . Is it . . . Are you going with a group of people?"

Silence stretches like taffy in the heat, longer than I ever thought was possible.

"She can go with me and Anabel like we planned," Danny says, trying to smooth things over and make up for his colossally badly timed announcements earlier.

"Right," I say. "Maybe we won't get the limo. Maybe we will. But I can wear this . . ." I look at my parents and do my absolute best to calm the situation.

"We?" my mother asks, as though she's never heard of that pronoun.

"We," I confirm. "Me. And I'll be asking Josie to go with me."

More silence. Then my mother must realize what I mean. "Deli Josie?" she asks, before my father can ask who the heck Josie is because he's terrible at remembering staff names and prone to avoiding names altogether, preferring "Hey there!" as his standard greeting.

"Yes, Josie who happens to work in the deli," I say as my dad looks at the tray in front of him, putting the pieces together.

"I see." Mom sits down and reaches for Dad's hand.

To their credit, they don't scream. They don't cry. But they don't tell me how great I'll look in the outfit either.

Danny steps up to the plate, ever the designated hitter. "Well, I for one can't wait to see you kick ass in that tux."

"Language, Daniel," my mother says automatically.

Danny reaches for a turkey roll-up and shrugs. "At the very least you can lend Anabel your jacket if it gets cold and I've managed to forget mine in the limo."

I give Danny a quick and thankful grin before joining my parents at the table. You can't expect conflict to go away on its own, so I don't want to duck away to my room even though it sounds like a refuge. My mother tips her chair back to reach the fridge and takes out a tray of premade lasagna. It lands on the table with a loud *clump* and she offers everyone the environmentally friendly silverware they're debating ordering for Giant Brookfield. We sit there, eating the noodles cold, right from the pan, as though not too much has changed. Like they haven't just been told their daughter is a lesbian.

I do wish my best friend were here eating rubbery lasagna with us. He always has a way of making things better. When we were eight and went trick-or-treating, Lucas had glitter in a water gun. He'd blast it on the sidewalks or in the air, showering everything around him in what looked to me, at the time, like magic. I breathe in hard, air catching in my throat. Where is that glitter now? But then I remember how it lasted forever, always turning up on my fingers or in my hair, glittery bits on my spelling tests or sandwiches, as though Lucas were trying to let me know he'd always be there. And maybe he will be. After all, I think as I swallow another mouthful of tomato sauce, Lucas is just angry. And he's just being a wounded guy. And how much damage can one guy do?

8

><

LUKE

Here is the problem with finding out that the person you thought was your best friend is in fact a liar who you never really knew at all: when you stop talking to her, you don't know which of her lies, if any, you're supposed to cover for.

When Tessa told me she was going to stop lying about who she was, I figured that meant she was going to stop lying to everybody. Because clearly I don't have any kind of special position in her life.

So when Sean Powter comes running up to me and says, "Dude, I just saw Tessa buying two Prom tickets. So who's the guy?" I don't pretend I don't know what the deal is.

"It's not a guy," I say. "It's a girl from Mason. Her name's Josie."

Sean stands there, mouth open, for about ten seconds, and then says, "Dude. That is not cool. I mean, I know she shot you down, but you shouldn't start rumors about her like that."

"It's not a rumor! It's the truth, okay! That's why she wouldn't go to Prom with me! She legitimately doesn't like boys like that. So she's going to Prom with a girl, okay?"

I half expect Sean to crack up, pointing and laughing at me, but he surprises me. He extends a hand and puts it on my shoulder—guys do not touch each other in our school unless it's to punch each other in the arm or bodycheck each other into the lockers, so this is a kind of special moment. "Dude. Wow. I'm sorry, man. I'm sorry I made— well, I'm just sorry." What Sean means is, "Your situation is now officially so humiliating that mocking you would be cruel, like kicking a puppy." He looks at his hand as if shocked to find it touching another guy, and quickly pulls it away. "See you at practice," he says, and disappears.

Maybe some stuff happens in the rest of the day, but I honestly don't remember it. I can't bring myself to pay any attention in any of my classes. I feel like everybody's looking at me, so I just kind of keep my head down and doodle in my notebook while my teachers and classmates drone on.

Normally when I'm having a bad day in the spring, I can think about baseball and look forward to practice. But even that's tied up with Tessa. We used to play on the same team, and when the trucks weren't unloading in the back of her parents' store, we'd practice there. I'd hit fly balls and grounders for her. And she taught me how to throw a curveball—the same curve that's had college and pro scouts at a bunch of my games this year.

My job is thanks to Tessa, of course, as is my sport. Without those things I've only got school. Mom will kill me if I bring any Cs home, so I do what I need to get by with a B– in every class but gym, which is an automatic A for varsity athletes.

All day I really want to tell Tessa how sad I am because she's the only person I ever tell about stuff like that. If I ever make the mistake of mentioning that to Mom, she goes on and on about how I have to toughen up, and if I think I have it so hard, I should try coming back to Brookfield in disgrace as a pregnant nineteen-year-old, blah blah blah.

But Tessa. Well, this is the part that hurts. For the kick-off of the season this year, we had a big father-son baseball game, which wasn't the first time I'd ever had to fake an injury to get out of something like that, but it was the first time it really bothered me. I went over to Tessa's to watch TV, and something happened on the TV—probably somebody said the word "Dad," and I just completely lost it. Crying like a baby about how I didn't have a dad, how mad I was at him for not wanting me, how mad I was at Mom for never even telling me his name, how there was this big hole in my life where most kids have a dad. And Tessa just rubbed my back and said, "I'm so sorry, Lucas. So sorry."

That is the only time I remember crying in front of

anybody since I got hit by a pitch right in the 'nads when I was ten years old. I showed that girl something I never showed anybody. She knew my true self, and it turns out I didn't really know anything about her. Nothing at all.

By the end of the school day, the lesbian rumor and the tuxedo rumor have converged, and the locker room falls silent when I walk in.

"So, yeah, I guess you're all talking about how the girl I asked to Prom is going to Prom in a tuxedo with a girl for a date. So go ahead and just get it all out of your systems now and tell me what a loser I am."

"So it's true?" Spence Harrington says.

"Yes, it's true," I say.

"Told you!" Sean says to Spence, punching him in the arm in a very manly and not-at-all homosexual way.

"Dude, that sucks."

"Yeah it does suck," I say. "And there will be kids from other schools there too. You don't think we're gonna hear about it at every game? God, she's such a selfish bitch!"

Out of the corner of my eye, I see Danny heading out of the locker room and onto the field. I feel a little guilty for a second, but only for a second. Tessa *is* a selfish bitch. I don't care if Danny hears me say it or if he tells Tessa. Because it's true.

— — — — — —

Apparently Danny does tell her because the next morning when I emerge from the doorway next to what used to be Hailer's Drugstore and step onto the sidewalk of Main Street, Tessa is standing there.

"What the hell are you doing?" she yells at me.

"Uh. It's called going to school," I say, and keep walking. Tessa puts a hand on my shoulder and spins me around. "Don't do that. I don't have to talk to you," I say.

"You have to listen to me. You owe me that after twelve years, Lucas," she says.

After all these years, I know that I'm going to lose one way or the other—once Tessa sets her mind to something, it's going to happen. So she's going to say what she wants. I may as well get it over with.

"What are you doing running around school telling everyone about Josie? Are you trying to hurt me?"

"Am *I* trying to hurt *you*?" I yell. People are driving by—not very many, since MegaMart killed the hardware store, the sporting goods/gun store, Al's Appliance, and the pet-supply store in addition to Hailer's Drugstore, but still—and staring. "How do you think I felt when I humiliated myself? Did it occur to you that that might have hurt me?"

And now she's crying. "I told you first, Lucas. Before I told anybody."

"Only because I put up a sign! And anyway, I'm pretty sure Josie knew before me. Unless you lied about that too."

Tessa clenches her fists. "You are really being a jerk, you know? Do you think this is easy for me? Any of it?"

"Is it easy for you? News flash, T—there are other people in the world who matter besides you." I'm not going to get a better exit line than that so I turn and start walking to school.

— — — — — —

School is buzzing—this is the biggest thing to happen in Brookfield since . . . Well, probably ever. Nothing ever happens here.

When I walk into school, I see a bunch of parents standing outside the office. I guess a lot of kids got suspended yesterday. Normally it would be weird that I didn't hear about something like that, but I'm not talking to anybody right now, so it doesn't really surprise me. Probably smoking weed out by the Dumpster. That's the usual cause of group suspensions. I go to my locker and find our second baseman Todd Alpert's little sister, Cindy, standing there. "Luke, can I get your opinion on the Prom controversy for an article I'm writing for the school newspaper?" she says.

I just look at her. "We have a school newspaper?" I'm not trying to be a jerk. It's just that I can't remember ever seeing one.

Cindy rolls her eyes. "It's been online-only for two years. Your picture is usually on the sports page," she says, her smile cracking a little.

"Huh. Well, yeah, I don't have Internet at my house." Cindy looks at me like she's waiting for the punch line. "No. Really. So what do you want to know?"

Cindy's smile is back, big-time. "I just want to know what you think about Tessa Masterson coming to Prom in a tuxedo with a female date."

"I don't care that she's a lesbian. I really don't. I just think it's so selfish. It means our whole Prom is going to be about her instead of being a normal dance. It's supposed to be a—it's like, be whoever you want to be, you know, I don't care, but you don't have to rub everybody's nose in it and make people uncomfortable. I mean, maybe some people won't even get to go to Prom now because of their religion, and I just think she ought to think about somebody besides herself and not do this."

Cindy is practically drooling over the juicy scoop she just got. "Great. Thanks a lot! Can I get a photo?"

"I guess." She whips out a little digital camera, snaps my picture and then goes running down the hall, and I forgot about it for the rest of the day.

So, apparently this is how it all gets started.

I really don't have Internet at home—our budget is pretty tight, and Mom has been very clear that she's "damn sure not paying forty bucks a month to bring pornography and videos of monkeys picking their butts into this house." We don't have cable either.

And I don't have a Facebook account or even e-mail, because we're not allowed to check Facebook on the school computers, and so if I wanted to keep up with that stuff, I'd have to go to the public library to use the computer, which is pretty much the same as hanging up a sign that says "Hey! I'm poor!"

Tessa tried to get me on Facebook once. "It's great!" she said. "It lets you connect with people all over the world, you know? People with different thoughts and ideas and perspectives!"

"Let's see," I said, and she scrolled down her page. I saw messages from all the people we go to school with:

New Jeans FTW!

Mom is on the rag ☹

Tyler tripped in the hallway today! LMFAO!

"Um," I said, "this looks like the same people with the same stupid thoughts and ideas and perspectives I see all day. Why the hell would I want to do this when I get home? Oh, hey, somebody's trying to chat with you."

She shoved me out of the chair, said, "That's private," typed something, and logged out. It was a couple of weeks till my birthday at that point, so I thought she was planning something and didn't ask any questions. Idiot. What else didn't I see?

So I go through life not really knowing what happens on the Internet. I guess I know in some kind of dim way that that article and the accompanying photo of me, being on the Internet, will theoretically be visible to the whole world, but why the hell would anybody outside of

Brookfield or Mason ever read the *Brookfield-Mason Regional Bee*?

— — — — — —

When I get to school the next day, I notice that the parking lot is full. This has never happened in the history of Brookfield-Mason Regional High School. There are cornfields outside of town that are smaller than our parking lot. When we host football games and our whole school and the other whole school shows up, you can still find parking even after the game has started.

Not today, though. The parking lot is full and there's a sheriff's deputy directing traffic. It's Jerry, known throughout the county as "the only cool one" because he will always call parents before resorting to locking a kid up for a drunk-and-disorderly or a speeding violation. God help you if you're DUI, though. I have it on good authority that the DUI cases not only get a suspended license and a night in jail, they also get a private viewing of the accident photos from when Jerry's little brother, Mark, drove drunk and killed himself and his girlfriend. There's a bench outside of school with their names on it.

Just beyond that bench, news vans line the street. Looks like Indianapolis and Cincinnati both made it here.

Along with a bunch of sign-carrying protesters. PROTECT OUR CHILDREN says one sign. NO PERVERTS AT PROM reads another. (If they were ever going to try to enforce that one, Prom would be nearly deserted.) STAND UP FOR FAMILIES reads yet another. What the hell is this?

I see a blond woman who might be hot if she were wearing two or three pounds less makeup standing in front of a camera. The cameraman counts down with his fingers and she starts to speak.

"Good morning, Cincinnati. Bridget Kelly reporting live from Brookfield-Mason Regional High School, where the culture wars are raging this morning."

I could keep listening, but I feel kind of sick. I've got that nauseating, called-to-the-principal's-office dread going through my body all of a sudden. What did I do wrong? How much trouble am I in? Why is there a culture war in Brookfield, Indiana?

I keep walking. I put my head down, but one of the sign carriers stops me. "Lucas?" he says. He's a red-faced white guy who looks like the collar of his white oxford is strangling him.

"Um," I say, "do I know you?"

"No you don't, son, but I know you. I want to applaud your courage for taking a stand for biblical values against the homosexual agenda." I just stare at the guy. I have no idea what the hell he's talking about.

"What do you mean?"

"Don't be shy, son. You're a hero. A real prayer warrior. Please know that the people of God are behind you in your struggle."

"Yeah. Well. Good to know, I guess. Listen, I gotta go. Don't want to be late to school." There are cameras everywhere, so I'm pretty sure at some point somebody's going to jump out of the bushes and reveal that this is all a hilarious prank.

"Like Daniel, he walks into the lion's den!" the guy yells. The rest of the sign carriers applaud as I walk through them. I've been booed on the field before. And it felt way better than this.

I walk into school and everybody stares at me. I thought I got a lot of attention for my sign mishap. I had no idea what a lot of attention was.

Jenny Himmelrath comes up to me and says, "I just want you to know I was wrong about you. You are a great person. Call me." Great. There's a shit storm raging outside that I guess I started, though I still don't really get how, but somehow this seems to have earned me a purity-ring booty call.

It also earns me this: I'm trying to walk to my locker with my head down when a shoulder hits me and sends me crashing into the lockers.

"Sorry," Danny Masterson says. "I didn't see you there."

I just look at him. I have no idea what to say. Should I say, "What the hell's going on?" "Why did you just do that?" "I didn't do anything?" I guess that last one's not true, but I don't really understand what I did or how I did it.

"You might want to watch your head at batting practice

today," Danny says. "My inside fastball's been getting away from me lately."

He walks away.

It's going to be a very, very long day.

9

Tessa

Stack 'em as high as you can without creating a fire hazard," my mother instructs as she wheels another flat of oversize pineapple-juice cans.

"You know I'll be lucky to get out of here without falling on my ass," I say, mainly to myself, but she overhears and gives me the store look, better known as the fires-of-hell look. When Danny went through a phase of sliding in the aisles in his tube socks or when I rolled up the sleeves of my polo shirt, we got the look. Only now it's hard to tell if the piercing gaze is only due to my cursing or if she wants any excuse to express her disappointment in me.

Left to the task of creating a sale pyramid, I methodically stack tins of juice with their labels facing out. Once the base is steady I have to use the stepladder and pretty soon I'm placing the few cans near the top—they're actually empty and just for display lest they bonk someone on the head and we get slapped with a concussion lawsuit. You can't be too careful these days, my dad always says.

I scan the store: shoppers buying charcoal for weekend barbecues, Britty Hailer studying the nutritional info on cereal boxes, a few parents whose kids run track or play ball, Josie at the deli, helping a guy with a huge sandwich order. The fans move the cold air around, the quiet hum from the frozen-foods cases fills the store like background music. Lucas always tried to figure out what note the hum was but since he has little music ability he never did. I adjust a pineapple-juice can so its green-and-yellow cheery label faces forward and nearly topple off my ladder when I see Jenny Himmelrath standing there with her hands on her hips, staring. It's the same stare she's been giving since fifth grade when she became obsessed with "weeding out the evil" in our elementary school and got people to sign a petition stating that they'd burn their Barbie dolls because they had boobs and suggestive clothing. In seventh grade she fully ignored her nickname, the Wrath, and took her place as the golden girl of the purity crowd. Her parties were legendary: elaborate make-your-own candy bags with stuff her parents would order online and arrange in glass jars after they'd rented out the movie theater for her birthday. Of course, they'd show *High*

School Musical every year because *Grease* was just too smutty. Later, there'd be chaste mixers in the Himmelraths' oversize barn, complete with themes—"The Wild West!" or "Party Like It's 1999!" or "Heaven on Earth," to which Lucas wore a shirt with #14 on it and walked around telling everyone heaven on earth was when Pete Rose played for the Cincinnati Reds. I laughed, but Jenny did not find it remotely funny because she wanted people in halos and cherub wings.

Now Jenny studies the cans of pineapple juice as though they are puppies who all want to go find a home with her but she hasn't made up her mind which to take.

"The display's not quite ready," I tell her, trying to prevent whatever poison is going to spew from her bright pink mouth, like I'm defending the puppy pineapple juices.

"Oh, I wouldn't dream of touching the display, Tessa." Her smirk is loud even from up high. I start to climb down, avoiding the pyramid lest I crash into it and draw more attention to myself. I've been trying to lie low the past day or so, just in case there's any reaction to me and Lucas. He's probably gotten some flak from the guys on his team, but it's hardly earth-shattering news, me not going with him to Prom. Josie went to a semiformal dance with a guy back when she lived in Philadelphia and he was cool with her "situation." She said he'd brought her a corsage and everything.

Jenny tilts her head at the cans and I'm about to open my mouth and tell her that the display is really sturdy, maybe even say something customer service-y like "Pine-apple juice has more vitamin C per fluid ounce than any citrus juice" even though I might be making that up, but Jenny stomps on my unspoken words.

"In the future, I wouldn't be caught dead buying any-thing from here." She pauses, waiting for the words to make their mark. "Your parents must be horrified."

Then she leaves me standing there in shock in the Giant Brooks that normally feels like a second home. I learned my alphabet by pointing to boxes of crackers and bottles of apple juice, drank beer with Lucas here, crushed out on Josie before she knew my name, helped sweep up glass crumbs from the break-in while my mom cried. I liked work. But now, with my stupid pile of cans and the overly chilly air, and Josie too busy piling honey-glazed turkey and Swiss to see that I am on my own here, I do what I've never done. I leave early, punch out, and retreat to my other home.

— — — — — —

This one's empty, too. Danny's playing a rematch against Northern, the team known more for their cheerleaders than for their pitchers, my mother is at a conference of refrigeration suppliers, and my father, knowing it doesn't get much more boring than guys trying to sell cooling supplies, is in Chicago for two days working the books and visiting off-site food plants. Over spring break he visited some plants and brought back a load of frozen ready-to-eat items for me to test and I invited Josie over, even though I was so nervous about it. She and I baked cinnamon buns, Cheese Twistees, which tasted like bark dipped in powered cheddar, and Sugar Knots, which were actually pretty good, and Josie laughed because I was so orderly about it all.

"Why do you have to write it all down?" she asked when she looked over my shoulder as I took notes on a clipboard. I hesitated, turning my head because we were standing so close I could feel her breath on my neck.

"Um . . . it's just what I was taught to do, you know, write down lists and be organized."

"Or," she said, "you could just enjoy the experience of trying all the stuff and then report back from your memory."

I turned to face her and knew then all the feelings I'd wanted to push away were rising to the surface. "What if I forget my reaction to each pastry?" I asked her, grinning. She put both her hands on my shoulders and said, "Or you could have some faith that the most important things will stay with you, right? I mean, how could you forget the incredibly chewy Sugar Knots?" And then she kissed me. And I asked her about the Prom and she grinned and nodded super-slowly, like she wanted the moment to last longer. And instead of being so nervous and shaky like I'd been with Ben, the lake lifeguard one summer, or Lyle Hughes, who I went out with for four months in freshman year but never touched, it felt good. I felt good. Right.

Now the empty house doesn't feel right. It feels hollow, or maybe that's just me. Normally, I'd call Lucas, punching the numbers without even looking because I've dialed them for so long. I'd only get out half a sentence before Lucas would say he'd be right over and we'd have a movie marathon or we'd go for a run and he'd be pissed because I'd beat him even though it didn't start off as a race. And maybe that's part of the problem; none of this started as anything competitive. It was a friendship. A best friendship. But now, since Lucas won't return my calls, it's like we're trying to prove who is more hurt: me because of him not being supportive when I told him the most personal thing ever, or him because he feels he was lied to.

It hits me hard, right in the middle of the living room, when I realize that I did. Lie to him. Even if it was because I thought he just knew, it's sort of unfair. Like when you tell your parents you're going to the lake with a certain friend, only you neglect to mention there's a group of boys going, too, who have no curfew, and maybe you also don't mention that you're camping there instead of sleeping at your friend's house.

I sigh, realizing I've still got on my dorky maroon Giant Brooks apron, and take it off and sling it over the back of the computer chair. If Lucas were here I could hug him and tell him I get it, the lying part. And he could hug me back. I sit down in the computer chair and debate going for a run by myself when I get a text.

JosieRosie: R U OK?

I hesitate writing back, knowing she must be on the clock and not supposed to be online except for Giant Brooks-related issues, cake orders and the like, but I type quickly, glad at least to have someone checking on me.

TessaM_13: Ya. Thnx. Missed school for much-needed "personal day"—hah! I'll B back for 2morrow's shift. No bigE.

JosieRosie: U R really brave.

TessaM_13: ?

Then I wonder if she means saying no to Lucas so I add.

TessaM_13: Can you imagine me in a gown? :)

JosieRosie: Um, ya...;). But really, u r weathering the storm.

TessaM_13: Storm?

I untie my shoes, feeling too tired to go for a run, while I wait for Josie's response.

JosieRosie: Not so much storm, hurricane. I'm here if U need.

— — — — — —

I'm somewhat baffled by her weather-related references. Sure, it's a pain, that my personal business is making its way around the Brookfield-Mason gossiping gabs, but storm? Hurricane? Did I miss something during my short absence? I shrug and cross my legs, first ignoring a framed photo of me and Lucas that catches my eye even though it has been here forever, and then letting myself stare at it. It's from the same era as the pictures he put on our senior pages—me with giant teeth, him with the front two still out. He lost his teeth late and used to ask me to knock them out so the tooth fairy would bring him a new baseball glove. How do you get from such simple times, when all you worry about is your teeth, to now? Maybe I'm not the answer to all of Lucas's romantic quests, but I could still show him a little kindness. I search online for the book he's been wanting about Ted Williams, some big coffee table book, a heavy and expensive one with years' worth of photographs.

But while I'm doing the online wander, I find two things that change my plans.

The first is that the book Lucas has been pining for is out of print.

The second is a link that leads me right into what Josie must have been referring to when she mentioned a hurricane. Only it's a Category 5, gale-force winds, and a volcano all at once.

Will One Girl's Choice of Date Cancel Senior Prom?
Brookfield Prom: Possible Cancellation Due to Lesbian Date
Indiana Teen's Infatuation Leads to Dashed Dreams

I click on all of them, each with explosive language, all with mixed messages that leave me slack-jawed. Canceling

Prom? They didn't even call me. Not that they have to, but still. According to to the *Indiana Banner*, "Parents are outraged," and are quoted as saying, "Tessa Masterson is making a mockery of a sacred tradition." Clearly they didn't quote *my* parents. Not that I know how they'll respond.

Of course, I want to retort with, "The 'sacred tradition' of stealing booze and barfing onto the Embassy Suites bathtubs and having sex loud enough for anyone in the halls to hear? Is that the sacred tradition you mean?" But I don't. I can't. Because just when I think I have my anger to hang on to, to cling to like it's a piece of debris from a shipwreck, I find another link.

The *Brookfield-Mason Regional Bee*!

BREAKING NEWS!

Brookfield, IN. Our small Midwestern community was rocked by the news this week that the entire future of this year's Senior Prom is being questioned due to one student's demand to attend the Prom with her lesbian date, both of them in suits traditionally worn by males.

The Brookfield-Mason school district has the right to cancel or alter school functions as necessary for the safety and wellbeing of the students and staff, and, according to Principal Hartford, "School policy requires that Prom dates be of the opposite sex."

Of course, this is not just an issue for one teen, but for all of the students at Brookfield-Mason who have been planning for the big event since last year, even going so far as meeting during the summer break to discuss themes and improvements. One student directly involved in the scandal is Lucas Fogelman: "I just think it's really selfish . . . our whole Prom is going to be about [Tessa Masterson] instead of just being a normal dance."

Tears are already streaming down my face, but when I read the last sentence, I just start sobbing.

"I mean, maybe some people won't even get to go to Prom now because of their religion, and I just think she ought to think about somebody besides herself and not do this."

There are umbrellas for rain. Parkas for blizzards. Storm cellars for tornadoes. But there's no protection for this. I close the search window where I had the Ted Williams book all ready to purchase from a used bookstore, put my head on the desk, and try to figure out what on earth to do next.

10

><

LUKE

What the hell were you thinking?!"

Mom is yelling at me. I have learned from long years of experience that one does not answer this question. Answering the question only leads to problems. The best way to handle this is just to sit back and wait for the storm to blow over.

"I don't even know where to start. It's like you've betrayed everything I thought I raised you to be! Friendship, decency, loyalty . . . Do any of these things mean anything to you?"

Again, not a question it would be wise to answer in any way. Mom takes a deep breath and continues, "You and I would quite literally be out on the streets if it weren't for the Mastersons. It's bad enough for you to throw your best friend under the bus because of a blow to your male ego, but for you to put that family at the mercy of the hypocrites who—" And here's where it gets weird. Mom stops yelling at me because she's getting choked up.

"I gotta get out of this house. I'm too mad at you to be here right now," Mom says, and off she goes.

So I'm all alone in a house with no cable. It's dark out, which means I can't go practice my pitches. It's not my night to work at the store, which means Tessa will be there, which means I really can't go there. And anyway I'm not sure the Mastersons are gonna want to keep me employed. If the boycott works at all, they're going to have to start cutting people's hours, and if I were them, I'd certainly start with mine.

And there's nowhere else in town I can go and not see a million people who want to talk to me, and I hate them all.

There are the people who think I'm a hero because I'm standing up for biblical values. Like I've ever opened a Bible in my life. Maybe if I did, I could find the part about how making a girl's life into a living hell is something that God thinks you should do.

And then there is the much smaller group of people who think I'm an evil jerk because I sold out my friend knowing exactly what was going to happen.

I don't feel like that's true. I actually sold out my friend not realizing or caring exactly what was going to happen. Which is better. Right?

The phone rings. "Hello?"

"Hi, this is Steve Gershon from the Cincinnati—" I hang up the phone.

A couple minutes later it rings again. "This is Wells Randolph Tarrow, chair of the National Organization to Defend Marriage—" *Click.*

Two more reporters call, and I just unplug the phone.

I turn on WLW and listen to the Reds game for a while. After four innings, Mom comes home.

"I'm sorry," she says. "I don't . . . Whew. My love for you is unconditional, which means I still love you when you're an asshole. But you've got to do something to fix this."

"I don't know, Mom. I don't know how to fix it."

"Neither do I, kiddo. But you've started this, and you've got to do something about it." She ruffles my hair and heads off to her room. Soon I hear the electronic beats of Miss Kaboom drifting out.

I try. I really do. I say this to the reporters outside school the next morning. "I just want everybody to go home and go back to not knowing Brookfield, Indiana, even exists. It's really . . . This is not that big of a deal, it's really not."

But then this question comes out of the crowd: "Have you been targeted by liberal activists? Why are you changing your position?"

"I'm not changing my position."

"So you still feel like it's wrong to have a gay couple at your Prom?"

"No. I don't think I ever said that. Look, I was mad, and—"

"So you're angry about what's happening in this town?"

I look at the crowd of people slavering for a good quote from me. I look over at the protesters with their antigay signs. "Yeah, I'm angry about what's happening in this town." I realize that they might use that quote to make it look like I'm some big antigay crusader, so I add this: "I mean, look. I don't know much about religion. So I need somebody to explain to me why God is going to get so angry about two kids who like each other dancing on Prom night. I don't go to church, but isn't loving your neighbor supposed to be part of the deal? So why are so many people so full of hate?"

I feel like everybody is staring at me all day long. I don't talk to anyone, and I guess I'm doing an okay job of giving off don't-talk-to-me vibes because nobody approaches me and tries to talk to me.

And then there's baseball practice. Despite Danny's earlier threat, nothing's really happened. But then again, Danny hasn't been pitching at batting practice since then. Until today.

As promised, an inside fastball "gets away" from Danny, and I have to hop back to avoid getting hit on the hip. The general chatter of practice stops, but I barely notice since I'm staring out at Danny on the mound. He's giving me a pretty good intimidating-pitcher stare. But I've got one of those too, so I give it right back to him.

It seems like a long time passes until Danny's next windup, but in pretty much no time at all after that, I'm on the ground with my batting helmet about ten feet away from me.

He hit me. In the head.

Baseball has rules, and one of them is that pitchers who throw at the head get dealt with outside the rules. Anybody who watches baseball knows this. Danny knows this. And even if he didn't before making varsity, he would have as soon as Coach Hupfer said this at our first practice: "Anybody throws at your head, you charge the mound. We'll take whatever happens, but every team in this league needs to know they can't intimidate us. If you let anybody throw at your head without throwing a punch at them, you're benched for one game and probably forever, because you're just not tough enough to play the game."

It's never happened, but even still, Danny's ready for me by the time I get to the mound. I still get in a hard shot to his face and he goes down. Then I'm on top of him, and the world disappears in a bloodred fury of fists and feet until eventually I'm being held back by three or four guys while another three or four guys hold Danny back.

I spit at him, and my bloody spit makes a little stain on his uniform shirt. "You gonna kill me? You wanna kill me? You're gonna have to do better than that!" I scream at him.

"This isn't over!" he screams back.

And then we're sitting in Coach Hupfer's office, and he's yelling at both of us about team unity, and about how he hopes we're happy with ourselves because we've each just earned three-day suspensions from school, which means missing two games, and about how we really need to think about the team before we think of ourselves.

"Masterson," he barks, "haven't you and your family caused enough trouble for this school yet?" Danny doesn't threaten to rip the coach's guts out, but he really doesn't have to; the look on his face is pretty clear.

And even though, yeah, I am a big—okay, huge—part of the trouble that they "caused," and even though I've ruined my friendship with Tessa forever, and am still mad at her, and even though I'm damn sure mad at Danny, I do bristle at hearing the coach bad-mouth the Mastersons.

"And you," coach says, turning to me. "I'm sure those scouts are gonna be a lot less impressed with your circle change when they see you're a hothead."

"Yeah, well, I guess I'm still better off than a fat ass with only one pitch," I say. Poor coach. Of course we've all Googled his stats. Even me, with no Internet at home. Three seasons with the single-A Quad Cities River Bandits in Davenport, Iowa, and each year his weight and ERA went up.

And now the coach doesn't have to say *he* wants to rip *my* guts out. "Get the hell out of my office," he says. "You both make me sick."

We walk out, and I see Danny fighting back a smile. Finally he turns to me and says, "I can't believe you said that."

"Yeah, well, I kind of can't either," I say. I'm about to

ask Danny if we're cool, but I know we're not cool. We'll probably never be cool again. But maybe he won't throw at my head anymore.

"Listen, Danny, I never . . . I never meant for any of this to happen. Will you tell Tessa—"

"I'm not telling her shit. You wanna tell her something, tell her yourself. You're pretty good at talking to people these days."

So I try. After Mom is through yelling (and yelling and yelling) at me, and taking away my Xbox that I bought with my own money, which hardly seems fair, I mope around all weekend and then, on Sunday night, text this to Tessa: "I'm so sorry." I get nothing back, and since I'm up till one a.m. waiting to hear from her, I decide to call.

"The number you are calling has been disconnected," a pleasant female voice tells me.

I finally fall asleep some time after that and am woken up what feels like about five minutes later by Mom blasting her music at four thirty a.m. before she leaves for work at the bakery.

"Mom! Miss Kaboom at four thirty in the morning!? Really?" I yell.

Mom pops her head in and says, "Oh, were you trying to sleep, my suspended son? I'm so sorry!" She flashes a grin but at least turns the music down. But not off. So I can't really get back to sleep until after she leaves, but once I've been up for half an hour, it's practically impossible for me to get back to sleep.

I thought it was going to be sort of cool to be suspended. I figured I would sleep in, lie around the house, play some video games, and, best of all, not have to see or talk to anybody for three days.

But Mom has ensured that I won't be playing video games (she took the cables to work with her! What mom knows enough to do that?), we have no cable, and I'm awake at four thirty in the morning.

Here's how bored I get: I read two chapters ahead in the American history textbook. I wind up doing a couple of days' worth of math, too. I'm actually thrilled to see Mom when she gets home because even fighting with her is better than solitary confinement.

And we don't really fight. She seems to be happy with the punishment she's exacted, so we watch an eight o'clock crime drama together and it's sort of pleasant.

She lets me sleep in the next morning, so it's seven thirty by the time I get up. I'm bored by eight thirty. And by nine, I'm really hating myself. I've got to talk to Tessa. Or at least get a message to her.

I walk over to the library, present my rarely used card, and sign on to one of the computers. I go to create a Facebook page, but I need an e-mail address for that, so I create an e-mail address. I guess I could just e-mail Tessa if I had any idea what her address is. I finally get my stupid Facebook account and search for Tessa but can only

find two Tessa Mastersons who aren't my Tessa Masterson. Or I guess I should say they aren't the right Tessa Masterson. So I can't send her a message that way. Facebook
suggests I join the "100,000 Strong for Tessa Masterson"
group. I don't know what that is or why it only has five
thousand members. It also suggests I join the "Indiana
for Traditional Values" group, which also has five thousand members. I log out of Facebook. I realize I have to
go talk to Tessa at the store.

I'm about to log off the computer when, just because
I'm sitting there, I search for "my best friend is gay."

11

><

Tessa

Someone wrote that war is hell. I'm sure it is and although I have no firsthand experience in the trenches or in tanks, I'm pretty sure high-school combat is second on the list of hellish places. At least it is for me.

I'm in front of my locker, which the janitors have stopped repainting because the last graffiti was in industrial-grade electric blue, and HOMO refuses to be covered over. From my bag I remove blue electrical tape and try to transform the last *O* into an *E* so it reads HOME.

"If this is home, get me the hell out," Spence Harrington says as he shuffles by in his flip-flops and shades. This merits a high five from one of his buddies.

I'm not used to the attention because I was always the girl off to the side. In class pictures, I never was front and center holding the black sign stating MRS. COBURN'S 2ND GRADE CLASS. And in track, I had the best times but I never bathed in the sports glory. I always thought this was because it didn't suit me—that I didn't need the attention like other girls, ones whose whole sense of self-worth was based on how many candids they got in the year-book, how many people voted for them for Prom queen.

But now, with my back against the cold metal of the locker and my eyes searching for a friendly face any-where, for anything that doesn't seem menacing or blam-ing, I'm pretty sure I don't want to be seen. That skulking on the sidelines and not taking credit for baking teacher thank-yous, not minding being cut from the paper in an article about local runners, even shrugging off Danny's thanks for the advice I gave him about applying early to MIT—it wasn't because I'm just so selfless and sure of myself. And it wasn't because I'm shy.

I'm a fly-under-the-radar person because all along I was afraid of being found out.

And now my secret is out.

Lucas stares at me from across the corridor, the class warning bell cutting the chatter. We lock eyes like long-lost lovers in a movie. People who are meant to be together.

Only we're not.

At Jenny's house, during one of her infamous parties (the theme was "God Is Great, So Are Games!"), we played hide-and-seek. We were fifteen or so then and all the games felt laced with tension: Would Marc try to slip his hand over Nina's during tug-of-war? Was Twister just an excuse to topple your body onto someone else's (answer: yes)? Hide-and-seek was sort of epic due to Jenny's land—sloping fields of corn and soy that scratched their own music in the wind, rocks that led to a dried-up creek, a barn in a state of disrepair and disuse complete with bales of hay and an old cart that I used to hide in. It was nice to get away there, listening to the country sounds and the laughter as everyone ran to find a place to duck, some waiting until the last minute.

I don't remember who the seeker was—maybe Jenny, maybe one of her minions. I just remember it took forever to be found. In the end, I wasn't. I had to crawl out of the cart and find everyone else, and of course I had bits of straw poking out from my hair. Meanwhile, everyone else seemed to be having a grand old time toasting s'mores. "Where were you?" Lucas had asked with marshmallow on his lower lip. Everyone at the party waited for my answer. "Waiting to be found, where else?" Turns out it wasn't hide-and-seek we were playing but sardines—everyone was searching for one hider. Each person who found the hider also got into the hiding place until they were all bundled in together, huddling and giggling and probably flirting and breathing into one another's ears, waiting. Only I'd been alone. "You totally missed out!" Jenny had said then, and when I see her now, next to Lucas, I know she's glad I'm fumbling with tape by myself.

"You coming to practice?" Melissa George's question

interrupts my memory as she pulls her math text out of her locker. She's not oozing excitement, but since she's one of the few people who'll talk to me I shrug and face her.

"I guess."

She zips her backpack closed with so much force I feel sorry for the fabric. "Don't bother," she spits.

A ripple of anxiety and anger comes over me. "Oh, God! Not you, too?"

Melissa turns on her heel, her sneakers squeaking on the linoleum. "Were you aware that I've had a thing for Spence Harrington since forever?" She doesn't give me time to say no, actually, I wasn't into tracking the crush-lives of my teammates. "No, probably not. And why is that, Tessa? Because you're self-centered."

At this point, Jenny pushes off from the lockers across the corridor, ignoring the late bell, and comes just close enough to Melissa that it's clear she's supporting her. Melissa sucks her breath in. "And just when it's all set, when Spence gets it"—she hits her head with her palm—"and he's going to ask me, maybe not in such a grand way with a neon sign or anything, but still. I had my dress and everything, Tessa. And now I can't go to Prom."

Lucas had a dog growing up, Mo-hee-to, because he couldn't say "mosquito," and right now Lucas has the same look on his face as he did that cold morning when Mo ran into the parking lot at Giant Brooks and ended up under a truck's back tire.

I don't know what to say to Melissa. I really don't.

Because I want her to go to Prom with Spence. I pause, knowing I'll be late for Spanish and will have to deal with more attention there—even bilingual taunts because Señora Aliaga doesn't care what we say as long as it's *en Español*. So I say, "Listen, Melissa. I want you to have an amazing time with Spence. It's great he asked you."

She stares at me like I've suggested it'll all be okay if she gets a pet kitty or something. "You are so totally out of it! Don't you get it? You're the whole reason I can't go to the friggin' dance in the first place. My parents have banned me from any activity you're a part of . . . and Prom? It's bad enough that you want to make the fashion mistake of a tux—that's just dumb. But airing your own private love-life issues is ruining the whole school."

I'm about to say sorry, cry, and run away, but I see Lucas still standing there, staring at me, at this, and doing nothing and I can't bear it any longer. My whole life is the sardines game again, and I don't want to hide and wait to be found. "Just so we're clear: if I go to Prom with a girl, a boy, or an antelope, it's no one else's business. If I wear a designer knock-off like Jenny or spend every last cent I've earned bagging groceries for an online extravaganza, it's no one's concern but mine. I'm not ruining the school. This isn't my fault."

I think I've made a difference. Covered up some of the verbal graffiti. But Melissa turns to look at Jenny and wrinkles her mouth at me. "Actually, the school student handbook says nothing about bringing livestock as your date, but it does forbid your lesbo plans."

Señora Aliaga pokes her head out from the classroom and yells at us in Spanish to get to our seats. Melissa and Jenny move. I just stand there. Did they really just suggest I take a cow or goat to my Senior Prom? I want to laugh, barf, and scream all at the same time. Lucas would come up with a word for that, the combination of all three. And we'd incorporate it into our daily lives like we did with IFA—Identified Flying Assholes. So I swivel, thinking I'll give it one last shot, and cross the impossibly wide corridor toward him.

Only when I do, he's gone.

I'm left there, alone in the echoing hallway, the getting-near-the-end-of-the-year debris strewn around me, my locker door with its paint and tape looking like a crime scene. And so not like home.

I rip the stupid tape off and resolve to try to be normal, only what's normal anymore? As I go to class with my head spinning, I hear the *click, click* of office assistant Mrs. Hayley's shoes on the floor. I turn, and sure enough, there she is, folding papers and sliding them into lockers where they wag like white tongues. I reach for the notice and try not to flinch when she doesn't make eye contact. Did she used to? Yeah, she was sort of friendly, wasn't she? I can't really remember now and I'm second-guessing everything.

I begin to shove the paper into my back pocket but then decide to recycle it, knowing Lucas would make me if he were here. Not that he is. Only when I unfold it by the green bin, I see that it's not an order form for extra yearbooks or a plea to come to the cheerleaders' carwash "fun"-raiser this weekend. It's an official notice from Principal Hartford detailing the "upcoming school board meeting to determine whether this year's Senior Prom and the events surrounding it will occur."

My breath stops. My mouth hangs open. Seriously? No Prom? No glitter ball, no fake waterfall at the Embassy Suites? No photos of students with carefully shellacked hair, and hands around the waist from the back? No updos or pedicures or virginity-losing in cars or hotel rooms? I scan the text dreading what I'll find, but the only reason given for the meeting is "necessary committee ruling" and "an issue affecting the entire community." But I know what they mean. When they say "issue," what they mean is Tessa Masterson.

12

LUKE

Everything I saw on the computer when I looked up "my best friend is gay" said more or less the same thing: your friend is the same person he's always been, it's just that you now know more about him. Also, don't worry that he's going to try to hit on you.

Of course my problem was more that the fact that Tessa's gay, or a lesbian or whatever, means she's never going to hit on me. It means the love I have for her in spite of everything is never going to be returned, at least not like that.

So, yeah, in addition to everything else, that kind of hurts.

But not as much as it probably hurts being Tessa right now. Of course I chickened out and didn't try to go talk to her at the store. Instead, once I got back to school, I just stood there in the hall and stared while awful people were awful to the girl I have considered my best friend for years. I kept seeing myself in my mind walking over there and putting a stop to the whole thing, but I was just so ashamed. I felt like I caused it. And Tessa was looking at me like I was one of them.

I guess maybe I am, but I never meant to be. Damn it. I should have gone over to her.

It's too bad Coach Hupfer doesn't have a speech for this occasion. Something like, "If you ever see douche bags picking on your friend and you don't stand up for her, you might as well hit the showers because you're not tough enough to deserve a friend."

We have a game after school, the first one back for both me and Danny, and the other team is nice enough to leave a complimentary copy of the DVD *Hot Girl-on-Girl Action, Volume 4: Slippery When Wet!* in the locker room for us. And the fans chant "hohhhh-mohhhhhs" in the cadence Red Sox fans invented in 1986 when taunting Darryl Strawberry with "Daaaaa-rryyyyyllll."

Of course the Red Sox fans were rewarded with one of the greatest chokes in sports history, and we take similar revenge on Brownsville County Regional Voc-Tec High with five shutout innings courtesy of yours truly and a sixth-inning grand slam from Mr. Danny Masterson.

The best part, though, is how the taunting from the other team and their fans pulls us all together, how the whole team stands as one.

Just kidding, of course. The team actually turns on Danny for being Tessa's brother and on me for, I guess, being her friend for years. Well, that and not actively joining in with the witch-hunters at school. Funny—I tried to stay out of it at first, but my failure to take either side just made everybody mad. Our teammates do not rally around us in the locker room to congratulate us. Nobody slaps me on the butt and tells me I had a good game. I guess they're afraid that might be too gay.

It's weird. Nobody's saying anything nasty to either me or Danny. They're just not letting us play in their reindeer games. Until we get on the bus, and I sit next to Danny in the very last seat, and somebody calls back, "Hey look! I guess they really do like it in the rear!"

Danny just drops his head. If I know his parents at all, they told him he wasn't supposed to get into fights over this stuff, that getting suspended just made it worse, and typical stuff that parents who've never been trapped in the back of a bus full of people ready to tear you apart say.

"Hey, these fags just carried your sorry asses through this game!" I yell. "Ten strikeouts, fifteen outs over here, and four runs from Danny. So maybe if you tried being a little less ignorant, your game would improve. How'd you do without us, anyway?" I know the answer: they got their clocks cleaned two games in a row.

Up in the front of the bus, Peter Davis yells, "I don't care. I'd rather lose than have to play with you fags."

I really want to yell at him. Or else hit him. But what's the point? The fact that I don't hate a lesbian has made me gay in their minds. There's no logic in what they're saying, so I can't argue them out of it. And I could take Peter in a heartbeat, but then what? He's still going to be filled with hate, and I'd get suspended again.

I'd like to report that I just quietly ignored them, but instead I said, "Funny your mom didn't think I was such a fag last night. Though she did ask me if I would give it to her in the—"

"Luke! That's it! Enough!" Coach Hupfer barks from the front of the bus. Yeah. Big man. He'll keep order on this bus as long as I'm standing up for myself.

The bus rolls past the MegaMart on the Brookfield-Mason line. The MegaMart corporation has bought a big billboard right across Route 126 from their store. It says: MEGAMART. STANDING UP FOR INDIANA'S FAMILIES. SHARING INDIANA'S VALUES.

Great. The Mastersons have held off MegaMart for years and I guess I always thought MegaMart was too big to notice them, but now that they see the Mastersons are down, they're making sure to kick them.

I hate MegaMart. I hate this bus. I hate this town. I hate this sport. I hate everything. Most of all, myself.

As we roll past Giant Brooks, I'm happy to at least see some new people with new signs in the parking lot. NO HATE IN BROOKFIELD, one says. GOD IS LOVE, says another. They're still far outnumbered by the people with the antigay, anti-Tessa signs, some of whom are screaming, red-faced, at the "God Is Love" people.

—— —— —— —— —— ——

Mom's waiting when I get home. She's actually cooked dinner. "Hey! How'd you do?" she says.

"Five shutout innings. Ten strikeouts. And everybody on the team hates me for, um, I guess being Tessa's friend or something, which I'm actually not anymore."

"Ugh. I'm sorry, kid. I'm afraid this is just gonna get worse before it gets better."

"Great. Mom, can I ask you something?"

"Sure. Ask me anything."

"Why did you come back here? I was thinking on the bus that the only reason I even want to keep playing baseball is that it's my ticket out of this dump. So, I mean, why'd you come back here, anyway?"

"Hang on," Mom says. She gets up from the table, goes to the fridge, and grabs a Miller High Life, cracks it, takes a long drink, and returns to the table. "Didn't realize it was going to be one of those conversations."

I pick up a forkful of taco casserole and chew. "Yeah," I say. "I guess it is."

"Okay. Well, honestly, I had no idea what the hell else to do. My whole world was completely upside down, and I had to start a new life as a mother at nineteen years old, and I couldn't ... Everything else was new, you know? Being a mom and everything. I couldn't face trying to start a new life in a completely new place. So I came here."

"But they were jerks to you when you got back."

"Some people were, for sure, including your grandmother, which is why we don't ever visit her in her retirement condo in Florida."

"I thought that was because we're broke."

"Well, yeah, that too. But also because, like a lot of other people, she couldn't wait to tell me what a horrible person I was and that I had shamed her and couldn't come looking to her for a handout. So, yeah, a lot of people were awful. But not everybody was. And, I mean, it was . . . I knew that even most of the people who hated me would look out for my little boy if they had to. I mean, I figured if you were born here, you'd be Brookfield-born, and Brookfield would look out for you in case . . . in case I couldn't."

I stare at her.

"Oh, Jesus, Luke, not like that. I wasn't going to leave you on the stoop of the fire station or anything like that. I was scared. You know? I was a year older than you are now. And I really didn't know if I was going to be up to the job. And if I was just another person in Cincinnati or Chicago or Indianapolis, nobody would care about you. But if I was here, I knew people who knew me when I was five years old wouldn't want my kid to suffer just because his mom was a screwup."

Mom takes another long pull on the beer, and since we're having one of those conversations, I decide I might as well go for it.

"So who was he, Mom? And why don't I know who he is?"

"Jesus, kid, you're really coming at me tonight. I thought you liked the taco casserole."

"I do," I say between bites. "I just need to . . . I need to understand."

"Well, I would go get another beer, but then the irony might be too strong. Honestly? I mean, I'm gonna give you this one last chance to not know some stuff about me that you're never going to be able to un-know. You know?"

"No."

"I mean, I'm gonna tell you some stuff about me that I'm not particularly proud of. And it's not the kind of stuff most kids like to know about their moms."

I take another bite of taco casserole. "Lay it on me, Mom."

Mom sighs. "Okay. I got to college after being . . . pretty sheltered. I mean, of course people in Brookfield were getting high and having sex nineteen years ago, but I wasn't one of them. First Lutheran youth group, academic clubs, homework, the library . . . Well, you know this type of kid now, probably.

"So college was a shock to me. Just the—it was too much freedom. For me. And I had kind of deprived myself of most of the fun of adolescence, so I was going to have as much fun as possible there. So I developed a kind of—I drank a lot. And other stuff. It's not hard for a cute naive girl to get her hands on any kind of intoxicants she wants. Or guys, for that matter. I'm not going to get into any more detail.

"But, okay, to answer your question, I guess, kind of, I . . . at the time, I figured it was my mistake alone, and I didn't want to blame anyone else. I wasn't careful or responsible. And, to be honest, it could have been at least . . . Well, let's just say there was more than one possible candidate."

I have stopped chewing my taco casserole. This is because my mouth is hanging open.

"And I just . . ." Now Mom is starting to cry and I feel horrible for even bringing this up. "I never thought about how it might affect you. I really . . . That probably sounds incredibly stupid to you, but I mean, I was a pregnant nineteen-year-old, so I wasn't that smart to begin with, and I really thought only about me. You were like, just an idea at the time, and I didn't want to . . . I'm sorry, kiddo, I really am. I screwed up, and I had my head so far up my own—I didn't even realize that the mistake that was gonna haunt me forever was not even trying to find out who your dad was."

It's awkward, but I scoot my chair up next to Mom and put my arms around her. "So. Only thinking about yourself with no idea how your actions were going to affect anybody else. I think I know a guy like that."

Mom laughs and wipes tears away. "What can I say. You come by it honestly."

— — — — — —

At school my access to the Internet is heavily filtered. But because I live in a small town my access to information, at least about Brookfield, Indiana, is still lightning fast. So, before I even get through the school door the next morning, I know that there's a big school committee meeting coming up so the community can discuss "the issue."

I called "the issue" my best friend for most of my life, and I want to go to her right now and tell her I'm sorry, and to be strong, and, oh yeah, guess what Mom told me about my dad?

I'm ashamed of myself, of how much I've failed Tessa, but I'm not going to add to the list of stuff I should be ashamed of every day. So I march up to Tessa's locker, where she is pulling books out and stuffing them in her bag as Melissa George and Stephanie Campbell have this conversation just a bit too loud right next to her.

"I feel bad for people who are, like, born defective," Melissa says. "But they shouldn't try to make everyone else miserable."

"Right?" Stephanie adds.

"So why are you?" I say.

"What?" Melissa says to me.

"Trying to make everyone miserable. I get how being born without a shred of compassion in your soul has probably made your life really cold and sad but, like you said, you shouldn't try to make everybody else miserable. Right?"

"Shut up, fag," Stephanie says, and she and Melissa turn on their heels and leave.

I turn to tell Tessa I'm sorry, but she's already walking away down the hall.

13

Tessa

People who don't run don't really get the art of it. Maybe that sounds too much like what I wrote in my essay for Northwestern, but while the blur of soy fields passes on my right, and with the unused red silo way off in front as my marker, I pound my feet on the pavement. You're not supposed to pound. Any distance runner will tell you that. Coach Branford basically implanted that in my head in eighth grade when I annoyed him every morning and jogged next to him in the hall and after school in the office until he let me join the high school team—practices only, but still.

There's poetry to running, and Lucas understood that. When we were little, we played snake 'n' follow, our own game, in which the leader runs a jagged path through cornfields or the town square or backyards, wherever we happened to be—even in the aisles of Giant Brooks where once there was an unfortunate incident with glass mustard jars and significant spillage. One of us would run or jog or take funny waddling steps and the other would have to follow; as the pace picked up, the harder it was, but at the end we'd wind up in a heap, laughing and out of breath.

My breath now comes out in gasps, not with the superb control I'm trained to have, no 'in through the nose out through the mouth,' just loud and gasping. The great part of running in Indiana is the flatness: you can see everywhere and nowhere all at once. So many afternoons or early Saturday mornings I spent scuffing these roads with my Sauconys, studying the abundant soy crop or watching the crispy-edged corn look ashamed in times of drought. And most of those times, Lucas was right with me.

He's not a runner. In fact, panting now with heat rising up my shins, my face prickling with sweat, I think about how little he complained about it. How he just did it. Followed me. How much of that was because he cared about our friendship and how much of that was because he was trying to woo me? If he were here now, I could ask. Or laugh about the word "woo."

But Luke isn't here. I start up again, my feet ticking their own lonely rhythm. He always kept up with me, even when I pushed hard and went too fast; it was like he was saying he'd never let me go on alone.

Josie's not into running. She likes swimming, but it's not warm enough for the lake yet and the nearest pool is almost an hour away. She's got a pass there and goes about five times a week. I've never been, mainly because she hasn't asked me. I'd go even though I don't like swimming that much. I'd go just to watch her butterfly the lengths and wrestle with her ugly green swimcap, which she displayed for me at Giant Brooks when no one was looking. We're not an official couple in that way, I guess. She does her thing, I do mine, and we cross paths happily. But it's not the closeness I had with Lucas. On the other hand, Josie's still up for going to the Prom, and even sent me links to handmade cuff links and cool earrings on Etsy.

The heat gets the better of me and I have to stop, hands on my hips, sweat pooling on my chest, between my shoulder blades. I cough. I'm at the intersection of Inlet 119 and Rural Route 2.

A Ford pickup scatters roadside gravel as it speeds by with all the windows down and kids from Northern in the back. They notice me and my heart pounds harder. But they don't stop and I'm horribly relieved, the kind of shiver you get when you miss a stair or nearly crash into the car in front of you. But two of the kids shriek from the back, "Lezzie loser!"

The words ring out over the fields, the flatness, and with my breath jagged and no one nearby, nothing looks beautiful. We don't even take the time to name our roads here—just numbered routes and inlets, highways.

I jog back alone.

— — — — — —

"Oh, no, she can't go!"

"Oh, *no*, she won't go!"

"Don't let one girl's sins ruin everyone's heaven!"

Giant Brooks has no employee parking lot, mainly because the store was built a long time ago when there were only two employees. Now there's just no space to add one without buying more land, which my parents have thought about but haven't done, feeling that people who work for the store like parking with the customers. And we all take the spots farthest away anyway. But no spot is far enough away from the chanting, the shouting, the clot of picketers in front of the glass entryway windows. Signs hung from inside boast charcoal on sale and locally raised pork, but outside the signs echo the shouts.

HELL WELCOMES TESSA!

The sign is large and painted in red, the drips probably unintentional but blood-like nonetheless.

I close my car door. My hand grips my rolled-up Giant Brooks apron, which I've brought in case I'm on sandwich duty, and I bite my lip hard as I try a running trick. If you look down, you feel like you're not making any progress, just the same road or track slipping under you and you get tired, or falter. But if you look ahead, try to pick something small and bright on which to focus way in front of you, you feel better, more sure. My parents urged me to stay strong and show up for work and I know they'd come out and meet me if I called them, but I don't want to. They've been supportive enough as it is. Last night when the phone rang for the billionth time, they simply unplugged it without a fuss.

"This is nice," my father had said when my mother produced an actual cooked meal and served it to all four of us. The windows were open, the spring evening breeze pushed through, and it was like hope was out there, somewhere. That is, until a smashing noise made us all jump and Danny lurched up right away, the king of reflexes, and stomped back in to show us the brick that had been thrown through the sitting room window. My dad cleaned up the glass and I had started to walk the brick out to the trash when my mom put her hand on my shoulder. "Don't get rid of it," she said. I raised my eyebrows, fighting tears that mirrored hers. "Let's use it." She had the same expression on her face that she did when the store was looted. "I've been looking for a doorstop, anyway." She pointed to the kitchen swinging door that's always driving the four of us crazy because it just won't quit swinging even after we've tried jamming a balled-up sock under it. She pointed with her chin so I took the brick—Dad and Danny were watching at this point—and I put it against the open door. We all watched, holding our collective breath like it really really mattered whether the brick stayed. Whether it could be something useful instead of something ugly. And it worked. Dinner was delicious.

Now I try to navigate what used to be a short walk from the parking lot to the Giant Brooks entryway; it feels marathon-length. I focus on the bright purple of a large cooler inside the store. Because people are gearing up for summer, my parents are heavy on the accessory sales to drive up the profits on the food. The purple cooler rests on top of a pile of similar coolers.

"You're the reason the devil himself is in our town!" a protester shouts in my face.

I suck the hot air into my lungs and it burns as I try to make my way across a line of picketers, each one with a sign: old ladies, mothers I've known forever, students from school, toddlers brought for show and who say in their lispy way, "She's bad!"

I nudge my way by a few sign holders but they jam together, purposefully elbowing me back toward the parking lot.

"Boycott Giant Brooks!"

This chant catches on and the crowd heaves with it. People won't buy things at my parents' stores? The purple cooler will sit there until fall. The milk will sour on the shelves. My parents will lose their house. Danny and I won't be able to afford college.

I try entering again, this time anger pushing me through the first line of people. I look for someone—anyone pro–gay rights, pro-me, pro-anything. But there's only anti.

"Queer is wrong! She can't go to Prom!" This one is said through a megaphone and I make the mistake of turning to see who is saying this and nearly get smacked in the face by Jenny Himmelrath's mother, tidy as ever in her pleated navy skirt and sensible flats, holding a giant white megaphone borrowed from Jenny's cheering squad.

"Wait—let me explain—" I start to say before Mrs. Himmelrath bellows into the megaphone again.

"Queer is wrong! Don't let her ruin Prom!"

I push past the rest of the crowd, the jostling and noise still overwhelming, until I hear, "You'd think she could try to come up with a better rhyme scheme. 'Wrong' and 'Prom' are really slant poetry and I think it'll be lost on mainstream Brookfield. We could've done much better, don't you think?"

I feel a hand on my back, basically pushing me through the protestors, guiding me past the signs of homemade hate, onto the automatic doorpad and into the store. "Lucas," I say as we leave the sticky loud air outside and come into the icy sterile store air. Saying his name gives me a shiver, makes me feel like reaching out and grabbing him, holding on or giving his hand a squeeze the way I always did at the end of a run, our eyes meeting.

And we stand there, both of us in our uniforms for work. I wait for him to open his mouth, for him to talk about pushing us both through the picket lines, about our overlapping shift today, to respond as the muffled protest-ers turn toward the window to make a show for us.

He opens his mouth to say something, and then a customer asks if the bratwurst is still on sale, and the moment's gone.

———————

"I smell like coleslaw," I warn Josie when I see her in the back half an hour later. Josie puts her hands on her hips, and I can't help but smirk.

She grins. "I always liked cabbage."

Her grin is only half happy; I told her about the brick. She couldn't see the strength behind using it as a doorstop, and we haven't spoken much about the picketers. Now her shift is over. She reaches for her time card and punches it in after giving me a half hug. Without speaking about it, we're not really showing any public affection. Not that a hug is such a big deal, but reporters are everywhere and I'm worried about the store. "I should probably make my exit," she says.

"Yeah," I say. I want to tell her something, or do normal things like ask her if she bought a dress or suit. And I feel torn between wanting to be the kind of person who doesn't care about what anyone thinks or does so I can run to her and we could at least have a quick kiss, or the kind of person I really am, which is the kind who is scared of doing the wrong thing many times over, the kind of person who is really good at trying to please everyone, even though now I realize I'm failing at that on all fronts: me. Josie. Lucas. The store. The town. My school.

"Here," Josie says, her small hands picking through her blue backpack in search of something. "I forgot to title it, which, you know, is like the cardinal sin of mix CDs, right? They have to have a name. But as usual I was running late today and there was paint on my car window, and . . ." She lets her voice get swallowed by the backpack as she zips it shut.

"Your car had paint on the window?" My shoulders fall with the weight of everything. What if I had just said yes to Lucas?

Josie brushes off the incident with her usual mellow confidence. "Look, Tessa, I let it go, and you should too, okay? A little vinegar and scrubbing and it came off."

I raise my eyebrows. "I was super-worried about the cleaning effort involved," I tell her, and tentatively take a step closer to her. She shuffles on the concrete toward me and, slowly, like we're testing tea that might be boiling hot, we hug.

We hear footsteps outside the door, and we immediately break apart, waiting for someone to burst in. But no one appears and we're left in a state of semiawkward post-hug closeness.

"I don't know if you're gonna like it," Josie says, and I realize that she's talking about the CD. I hold it, spinning the shiny silver object as though it's a world I can escape to. "Billy Bragg? 'Milk of Human Kindness'?" She shrugs.

"'Greetings to the New Brunette'...Anyway, maybe you will. It's a little eclectic."

"I'm good with eclectic," I say, and wish we could go hang out somewhere and listen to it together. Then it hits me that I can say this, so I do. And she nods.

Just for a moment, I can see it: us on the floor of my room, the music spinning us into some sweet orbit, my mom cooking something in the kitchen, the scent wafting up—or, more probably, reheating some deli oddness she brought home. And then I flinch, knowing that in my scenario, Lucas was there, too, listening with us, delivering his commentary on each song.

"You must miss him," Josie says, reading my mind.

I nod. "Everything's such a mess—your car, the people out front . . . Prom? All this about Prom?" I wonder if Josie had a song she wanted me to request for her at the DJ station. If there's actually a dance somewhere that allows people to just wear what they want or bring anyone as their date.

But it's not here. And it's not going to happen for us. Even over the air-conditioning's hum, I can hear the muffled protests. So I don't ask her what song she wanted to dance to with me, or how she was going to wear her hair. Since all of that is going up in flames, and if the town has it their way, I will be, too, I just tell her, "Maybe you want to go the back way? Behind the Dumpsters?"

Josie nods. "I never meant for this to happen, you know," she says when she's at the door. The burst of sunlight surrounding her is almost eerie. "I just needed to find a way of earning a few extra bucks."

"I know. Me neither."

"I'm gonna duck out," Josie says, and hunches over as though about to be ambushed.

I watch her go. I can't believe what my life has turned into.

"Seriously? You're letting her slum by the Dumpsters? Those things haven't been emptied for two days—the collection truck couldn't get past the crowd." Danny hangs up his baseball hat and tries to fluff out his hair in the small service-room mirror.

"How else should Josie get out of here? It's insane out front," I say, and march over to the deep soapstone sink that is leftover from when this store was one tiny general mercantile. The faucets squeal as I lather my hands, trying to smell like soap instead of mayonnaise.

Danny sits on the bench. "You know, it is possible that everyone out front is full of crap."

I turn to face him, my hands dripping onto the concrete floor. "Look, my life sucks right now. I can barely make it into work without getting my head ripped off. Mom and Dad won't have a store to go to if it stays empty like this, and all because of what—me? My dumb idea to, I don't know, actually be honest?" I shake my head.

Danny stands up, scratches his head, and then takes me by the shoulders and sits my butt down on the bench. Employees' street clothes hang on pegs behind me, empty memories of who they are outside of their deli, bakery, and cashier roles. I raise my eyebrows at Danny. "I'm on the clock here, buddy. Potato salad is my future."

"But it's not!" Danny cries, like I've denounced all that is good and holy about grocery items. He clears his throat. "Okay. Here goes." He studies my face. "I'm going to assume for the time being—correct me if I'm wrong—that you don't know much about European football."

"If by 'know' you mean 'care'...." I grin.

"Shush. Listen. It's 1988 and—"

"And we're not even born?" I interrupt.

"God, how did Lucas put up with you for so long?" Danny mutters, a smile playing on his lips. Hearing Lucas's name makes my heart curl up on itself, and I flop back against my dad's old barn jacket.

"Fine. I'm listening, oh, wise one."

Danny claps his hands. "It's 1988 and Wimbledon Football Club pretty much sucks. They're sort of laughingstocks all across England, right? No one takes them seriously when they show up for the massive final competition at the FA Cup final." Danny grabs his deli apron and slings it over his head, tying the strings as he has a million times before. "The point was the team did their own thing—they were wild and played jokes and the head of the team was this guy Samir. Everyone thought he was bonkers. Wacko reputation for setting things on fire or letting other players do that." Danny laughs. "Once the guy even offered to buy the striker a camel if he scored a certain number of goals."

"Are you saying you're going to get me a camel?" I ask,

and stand up so Danny and I are face-to-face. "Because that might really help me right now, you know, riding— really slowly, of course—to school on a dromedary. Talk about blending in."

"No, see, that's *not* what I'm saying. You don't blend in, Tessa. You kind of did before but only because you exhausted yourself doing it. And now your cover's blown. You can't get it back."

I bite my lip, the refrigerated air cooling my limbs.

"Everything that came before, it's sort of gone. Or changed. So trying to do your duck-and-cover thing, it won't work. Samir let his team be themselves—do what they liked. Create their world. Havoc, heaven, whatever. Everyone wrote them off, Tessa. The paper called the whole team crazy. Turns out, all those jokes and crazy times made their team stronger. They crushed Liverpool, who totally dominated back then, and Wimbledon's goalkeeper, Dave Beasant, was a hero."

"I've never heard of him."

Danny grins and crosses his arms. "Right. Because you can be a hero in your own tiny football pitch or Mid-western town and not fight everyone's fight. Don't make this into a world issue. That's too hard. Think about you. Tessa. The runner. The girl who applied to college a decade early beause she was too excited to wait. The friend everyone can only dream of having. The girl who bought a kick-ass suit to wear to a really fun dance."

"Team spirit?" I ask. I picture the tux hanging in the dark of my closet.

Danny nods and laughs. "You're totally picturing the tux right now, aren't you?"

"I hate that you can read my mind," I tell my brother.

"I hate that they're doing this to you. To us," Danny says, and hands me a bottle of tepid seltzer from the supply crates in the corner.

I guzzle it, the bubbles choking me, and then look at Danny and start to laugh, which makes me choke on the water even more. "What if," I gasp, as I try to regain my voice, "what if I went anyway? What if I go to the meeting and just . . . I don't know . . . tell them too bad. They don't get to decide who I dance with. Or what I wear."

Danny gives a big baseball team *whoop!* and punches the air. "Yes! That's what I'm talking about!"

My voice rises. "I mean, the meeting is open to the public and it's tomorrow. Which gives me ten hours to feel nauseated and anxious and almost entirely alone."

"But not completely," Danny says. His face is bright. His plan worked.

"I know," I say, and thank him with my eyes. "And yes, you are the king of the sports pep talk."

"Go Wimbledon!" Danny shouts, and puts his hand out.

"Go Wimbledon!" I shout back, and slap him five, already questioning whether I'll make it into that school board meeting—and, if I do, if I'll make it out alive.

———————

The night inches forward, my digital clock ticking minutes away, then, finally, hours. I get dressed quickly, throwing myself first into a jean skirt, thinking the skirt might make me seem less . . . I don't know . . . less butch? But then I get annoyed at myself and my sticky closet door and step out of it and into the standard spring wear of nearly every high school girl here—jeans and a tank top. Before I can renege on my outfit or overanalyze whether flip-flops are too casual or sneakers too manly, I fling my bag on my shoulder, take the stairs two by two, and grab an unheated bakery-case leftover (read: stale) sticky bun to eat in the car.

As I drive—a little too quickly—toward school, it's like I'm seeing myself from above, an aerial shot of a girl— any girl—driving through small-town America. And I know the girl isn't just any girl. It's me. But what I notice about the streets that I've been walking and running and driving on forever is that they're just strips of overlapping fading tarmac, all running into one another. No matter which way you go, you wind up in the same town. The same place. I pull into the school lot, sheltering myself against the shouting and car horns directed my way, all the while realizing that, like it or not, I have to be here, doing exactly this.

So I ignore the "freak" taunts and the graffiti someone thoughtfully nail-polished onto my tire, which I only just notice now, and give up looking for sympathetic gazes as I go to the principal's office. Usually, the industrial gray carpet and ancient desks and yellowing calendar give off an air of serenity. At least they have for me, because I'm not someone who gets into trouble—I've only come here twice: once when my grandfather died and Mrs. Glickerman, the secretary, had called me down in the middle of World Culture to tell me, and once to discuss the food my parents were donating to the graduation reception—that was before MegaMart took over all school functions, with their gummy guacamole and shoelace-flavored straws.

"Ms. Masterson," Mrs. Glickerman says, her eyes on her desk as though something terribly important has glued her gaze there.

"Yes, hi," I say, and pinch my thigh through my jean pocket to keep myself from running out. "I'm here for the meeting?" Damn, why'd I make it sound like a question?

"I'm afraid it's a closed meeting." Mrs. Glickerman shakes her head.

I'm about to get frustrated when I remember my training. Customer-service practice. I take a breath. "I hear what you're saying—this meeting isn't intended for students." Mrs. Glickerman nods. "However ..." She looks up at me, suspicious. "Technically, it's an open meeting because it concerns a community event, meaning one that takes place not on campus but at an off-site location ..." I lay it on thicker. "I really appreciate you giving me the heads-up, though, because it's so much better for us all to be informed of these things, and you really play a large part in this school and its day-to-day functioning ..."

She motions for me to proceed to the principal's door,

which feels like a triumph until my hand palms the dirty brass knob and I feel the full weight of the door, and of everything beyond it, falling on me.

We get past the introductions and before the parents can stone me to death or drag me away, the principal uses her arms and voice to shush everyone. Once, Lucas and I went to farm camp and we had to wrangle sheep. We were so busy laughing and goofing off in the hay, we didn't get our chores done. Our penalty was missing the afternoon milk shakes and having to catch this insane lamb who was tiny but fast. Lucas and I cornered it. Now I know how that lamb felt.

"The educational process is a delicate one," Principal Hartford says, her face chalky, lips outlined in brownish pink. I hear murmurs of agreement around me. My pulse quickens, sweat beads on my upper lip. "All students have rights."

All students do have rights, I think. Could it be that Principal Hartford is actually on my side? My hopes rise as the air in the room grows thin.

"What about the rights of our children?" asks one parent.

"Exactly," says Lewraine Abernathy, the superintendent. She nods at Principal Hartford.

I wish for what feels like the fiftieth time that Lucas were here. Or Danny. But I remember my brother's words. Wimbledon. I cough, but before I can speak, Lewraine takes over.

"Your"—she gestures loosely at me as if addressing the air in front of me—"actions of late are very distracting to the student body. It is the belief of the school board that hosting a Prom under these conditions is not in the best interest of the school."

I think about Lucas and his Prom-invitation sign, about my brother and his girlfriend, about everyone, even the small-minded assholes in the hallway misspelling "homo" so it reads "hommo" on my locker. "Everyone deserves a fun dance," I say quietly.

Clearly, these are the words they've been waiting for.

"We're so glad to hear you say that, Ms. Masterson," says Principal Hartford.

Up until this whole thing started, I was Tessa. Now it's more formal. Did lawyers tell them to call me that? Or are they so grossed out by me they need to distance themselves even through what they call me? Like I'm not still the girl they knew on the track team last year.

But I am.

"I deserve a Prom, too," I say, this time a little louder.

"That's fine," Lewraine Abernathy says, in a tone like she's hushing a toddler. Jenny Himmelrath's parents are there and they add a few yeses and then Mrs. Himmelrath bursts in.

"You could have your own Prom, dear."

I raise my eyebrows, shocked and annoyed. "I—"

"The bottom line is that we've taken this very seriously, Ms. Masterson," the principal says. Like I've been treating it so lightly, right? "And we have determined that district policy leaves discretion up to us. Neither do we agree to your bringing a same-sex date to our Prom nor do we give you the right to wear clothing specifically designed for males."

The customer-service me knows that I should give in on a couple points. Find a compromise and make it clear we're all on the same page.

The customer-service me has left the building.

"So, basically, you're telling me I can come to the Prom—"

"No, we're saying the oppos—"

"Wait," I say, "I'm not finished. You're saying I can come to my own school's Prom if I decide to go with a date of your choosing . . ."

"We're not exactly telling you whom to choose . . ."

"That's not really the case. You're saying girl dates are off-limits, but any boy I want to bring is fine. Correct?" They actually nod. "So you guys get to choose who my Prom date is . . . and you get to choose what I wear! Wow. There's personal shopping and then there's this." I draw a breath as Mrs. Abernathy reddens and begins to raise a hand to slap on her knee.

"Ms. Masterson . . ."

"Tessa. I'm Tessa."

"Well, Tessa, this isn't up for negotiation. There's been a vote."

A chill washes over me in the stifling office but I stand

tall in my flip-flops. Is this the kind of thing people sue over? I'm in way over my head. I picture how calm my dad was cleaning up the glass the other night. How strong my mom was about the brick. I can't back down. "And just what happens if I show up at your beloved Prom anyway?"

I clench my hands, hoping one last time they'll come to their senses and support me. The student, not the issue. I think about Lucas bursting through the picket line with me and wonder what he would have said if he'd had the courage to talk.

"Oh, you can show up." Mrs. Himmelrath smiles like she's offering arsenic in a champagne glass.

"But if you do, you will be expelled." Principal Hartford looks at me long enough for me to know this is the end of the meeting. At least for me.

I walk slowly to the door, my shoes slapping the tight gray carpet that has felt a thousand shoes on it over the years, tons of kids who know they've messed up and are being punished for it.

Only I haven't done anything wrong.

So I stop and pivot. "Thanks so much for taking the time to discuss all of this!" I say brightly, in my best customer-service pitch. And then, "I hope Prom is exactly what you hope it will be." They all seem relieved until I add, "I'll see you there!"

14

><

LUKE

I'm at the library again. TESSA MASTERSON **WILL** GO TO PROM is splashed across the *Bee's* Web site. In an exclusive interview with Tessa, reporter Cindy Alpert reveals that Tessa has been threatened with expulsion if she shows up at the Prom with (a) a female date or (b) a tuxedo on. Since Tessa's determined to do both, I guess they're going to have to double expel her or something.

I click over to Facebook. "100,000 Strong for Tessa Masterson" now has 8,024 members. I click the "like" button and make it 8,025. I'm not the greatest student in the world, but I have paid enough attention in English class to recognize irony. If there's anybody on earth who hasn't been strong for Tessa Masterson, it's me. But maybe I can change that.

Maybe I have to. I go to work, where Josie looks at me like I'm the worst person on the planet, which pretty much reinforces what I'm feeling. And the Mastersons, on those rare occasions when I actually see them, look right through me. Again, I feel like I deserve that and it's preferable to them firing me, which is probably what I would do in their shoes. But, as we've seen, I'm just not that good a person. I feel okay while I'm working, but then when I take my mandatory fifteen-minute break, my life starts to feel really heavy, and I sit in a plastic chair that's probably as old as I am, with my head on the folding table. At some point, Kate Sweeney walks in, and eventually I notice her.

"Hey," I say.

Kate looks at me. "Are you okay?"

"Nope," I say. "I screwed up worse than I ever have in my life."

Kate smiles at me. "Well. Knowing that puts you ahead of most people."

"Thanks. I feel like the stuff shit scrapes off its shoes."

This earns me a smile. "I don't think you're quite that bad. You're a lot cuter than shit."

I laugh. "And you look better than barf. Hey, are you working tomorrow? I kind of—I think, like, everybody here hates me and everybody at school hates me, and it's just nice to see a semifriendly face."

Kate laughs out loud. "Semifriendly. That's what they call me down at the truck stop. But, I mean, I'm not working tomorrow. Or, I guess, for the rest of the summer. I just got laid off."

"What?" I'm a little shocked.

"Yeah. It turns out when people can go to MegaMart and pay less money and not have to face down a parking lot full of psychos—"

"Have you ever been in the MegaMart parking lot?"

Kate laughs. "Yeah, okay. Point taken. But the psychos in that parking lot are not organized and holding signs. Anyway, I was pretty much of a charity hire, so with business in the toilet, they can't really afford to give me three shifts a week anymore."

I feel like all the air has gone out of my lungs, and my head somehow winds up on the table again. Everybody for two counties knows how loyal the Mastersons are to the people who work for them. It's not just my mom—tons of people have stories of paycheck advances that got them through a tough divorce, or pallets of food that mysteriously appeared outside their trailers in the middle of the night when times were really tight. It's one of the reasons people shop at Brookfield Giant even though they can save money shopping at MegaMart.

And now the Mastersons are laying people off. Or at least one person, though probably there will be more, if there haven't been already. This, too, is my fault. I can't believe what I did by shooting my mouth off. I just want to curl up somewhere and quietly die.

"You okay?" Kate asks me again.

"I . . . Are you gonna have enough money for college?"

She puts a hand on my back and bends down next to me, smiling. She smells good. "Yeah, Luke. You didn't ruin my life."

"I just . . . I can't believe how bad I screwed up."

"Yeah. Well. How are you gonna make it right?"

"I don't know if I can. It's too big. It's too much."

"It's big, but it's not too big. And you're not alone. There are a lot of us in this town who aren't—like that. I think a lot of people are just waiting for someone else to say something sensible."

"Well, I think I've proven that saying something sensible isn't exactly my strong suit. But I guess I'm gonna go for it. The school board is meeting tomorrow night," I say. "You know, because they couldn't convince Tessa to change her mind."

"Oh, I know. It's gonna be broadcast on local eight cable access! I never miss one!" I stare at her blankly. "I'm totally kidding. But I am gonna watch this one. Or maybe even come."

— — — — — —

I have never had much trouble sleeping, except when Mom wakes me up blasting Miss Kaboom. No matter what kind of big game I've had, or big test, or big paper due, or anything, I've always been able to pretty much lie down, roll over, and fall asleep. But tonight, after sixteen rolls in various directions, I'm still awake. I turn onto my back and stare into the darkness—well, the pale yellowness, really, from the streetlights along Main Street that light up the street where hardly anybody drives anymore and the sidewalk where no one ever walks. I'm nervous about the meeting. What if I get up there and can't say the right thing? What if I do say the right thing and I've still lost Tessa's friendship? Would I forgive her if she'd done something like this to me? And what happens to me and Mom once I plant my flag in the sand and announce once and for all what side I'm on?

Well, no booty call from Jenny Himmelrath, that's for sure. It's not like I care about that, though. I mean, yeah, I am a guy, but the idea of kissing one of the people who thinks Tessa's evil actually makes me kind of sick.

I guess my problem is that I just can't imagine what comes next. This isn't a feeling I'm used to, or one that I've really ever had before. I mean, you live in a town like this, you pretty much know what's happening next. It's not like you ever start a new school where you don't know anybody. You can always imagine what the next day, the next week, and the next month will be like, because they're going to be pretty close to what the last day, the last week, and the last month were like. But not now. Now Tessa's in completely unmapped territory, and if I'm going to be able to look at myself without completely hating myself, I've gotta go stand there with her.

It's scary.

So I don't sleep.

At around four, I get up, go to the kitchen table, flip open a notebook, and start writing out what I'm going to say to the school board. At four thirty, Mom staggers toward the coffeemaker. "Hey," I say.

"Yaaah!" Mom yells. "You scared the crap out of me! Well. I'm awake now. The question is, why are you?"

"Writing my statement for the school board."

"Lemme see."

Mom grabs the notebook and reads it while she busies herself with the coffeemaker, and when it starts to gurgle, she turns back to me. "Coming off the bench, huh? Getting in the game at last?"

"I guess so. You think it's okay?"

Mom walks over and puts a hand on my shoulder. "I think it's wonderful. I think it's the single best thing you've ever done. And it makes me so proud of you I could just explode right here."

"Don't do that. The cleanup would be a bitch."

Mom laughs as she pours coffee into a twenty-ounce travel mug. She takes a big gulp of coffee and says, "All right. I'm outta here. You know every yahoo for a hundred miles is going to turn out for this thing, so you'd better get there early if you want to be able to speak."

"I will."

"Good deal. I'll see you there."

— — — — — —

The school board meeting starts at seven. I get there at four thirty, threading my way through the news trucks and reporters with perfect hair and too much makeup, and some female reporters too, and I'm not the first in line. I'm not even the twenty-first in line. I don't know what number I am. I can't really see all the way up to where the line starts. I'm hoping Tessa is up there somewhere. Even if she's not, I know she'll hear about me being here, but I really want her to be in the room. I really want her to see me put myself on the line for her so she knows it's for real. I really want her to forgive me, though I guess I won't blame her if she doesn't.

People look at me while I'm standing there. I'm wearing my Brookfield-Mason varsity baseball jacket over my T-shirt. I kind of imagine they're wondering what I'm going to say, which side I'm going to be on. Well, most of them are wondering that. At five forty-five, Mom arrives and takes her place, way behind me in line. She looks at me and gives me the thumbs-up. I reach into the pocket of my jacket and feel the folded-up pieces of paper that hold my statement.

At six o'clock, a bald guy with glasses wearing a white short-sleeved button-down shirt comes out and tells us that, due to time constraints, the school board is not going to be able to hear from everyone. "The meeting is scheduled for two hours. That means that after initial announcements and other business, there will be time for exactly forty-five people to speak. Each person will have no more than two minutes. After two minutes, the microphone will be turned off, and those who refuse to leave will be escorted from the building by deputies from the

Clay County sheriff's department. I will now hand out numbers to everyone who will get to speak. Those who do not get to address the board are welcome to submit their comments in writing after the meeting."

The guy walks down the line handing out numbers, and I get nervous because I'm not sure how far back I am. When he gets to me, the guy hands me a card with the number 39 on it.

And then I get even more nervous. Because now I have a number and I have to do this. I start getting sweaty even though it's not very hot. I feel like the other people in line should be staring at me because my heart is pounding so loud. My stomach feels sour, and I burp a nasty echo of the hot dog I had for lunch.

At six forty-five, the door to the meeting room opens, and we all start filing in from the hallway. Those of us with numbers get to sit in the first two rows.

Tessa is right up in the front, talking with some old guy I don't recognize. I want to get up, go over to her, and say, "Tessa, I'm sorry for being such an idiot." But sorry doesn't cut it with something like this. You've got to do something bigger than that to try to make it right.

At seven o'clock, the school board chair bangs the gavel and calls the meeting to order. It's time to make it right.

15

><

Tessa

If you've never been to a school board meeting, the one word that usually sums them up is "boring." Mostly the school board works through funding issues, space issues like where to put the modular classroom so Brookfield-Mason can actually have a foreign-language program, or they nod as parents complain about the late bus that has to double back across two counties. It's pretty much all monotone voices and the shuffling of feet, people who can't wait to get out of the airless room and go home for dinner or to watch *Monday Night Football*. When my parents were contracted for providing dinner, back before there was even industrial food distribution around here, Danny and I were dragged to every meeting and left in a corner to do homework or fend off the urge to fall asleep while the grown-ups talked. No one noticed we were there.

And now I'm the one everyone has come to see—the circus-sideshow freak who not only isn't a cheerleader but is the cause of all things bad in this town.

A couple of nights ago the doorbell rang and I poked my head out of my room, sure it was someone picketing or burning something in our yard. But it wasn't a burning that I smelled. It was pigs in a blanket, the kind we've grown up on because Giant Brooks makes them by the platter. Downstairs my parents had set out trays from each of the specialty departments of the store: deli, bakery, cheese case, fruits 'n' veg.

"What's the occasion?" Danny asked before I could. He swiped a handful of pigs in their blankets, disturbing the careful fan arrangement my dad had made.

"Well, it appears we've got a visitor!" My mom's furrowed brow was accompanied by a smile as she let in a man in a suit that I was pretty sure didn't come from Mr. Tux. He actually shook my hand, which no one had done in ages.

"I hear you've got a bit of a situation," he'd said. I nodded. "I'm Bill Wekstein. I'm from the ACLU, the American Civil Liberties Union. We protect people's constitutional rights." He talked. We listened. I talked and he listened to me.

"So you'll be at the meeting with me?" I asked, and Bill nodded. My parents signed some legal forms and for the first time since maybe this whole thing started, I felt like we had a sort of team.

— — — — — —

But tonight, I'm not so sure. The normally airy space is jammed with bodies, each one tense, the talk is heated, and it's impossible not to overhear specific words: "ridiculous," "troublemaker," "sinner," "ruining everything," "dyke." And it's impossible to ignore that the words are meant for me.

How can I not feel crushed? These are people I've known my whole life. Lucas and I used to stack up all the cushions from his couch, gathering extra pillows from the bedrooms, blankets, anything, and see how difficult it was to stand on the stack, how much we could pile up. And it always felt good being crushed by the soft pillows, and even better to stand up out of them and feel free and light. Only this—the stares that pierce me, each face directing anger toward me, even formerly nice people like Misty Schiclione, whose locker used to be across from mine until she started avoiding me, and Topper Martin's parents, who sold my parents their house—this isn't the pleasant weight of blankets and cushions. This is hell.

My arms stick to the chair's old wooden arms and I turn to peel them off, looking for my parents, for Danny, for anyone to give me reassurance. The local police are in full force, along with reporters and herds of gawkers. The double doors are open but so crammed with bodies that no one is getting in. Way behind, through the window, I see Danny's baseball cap and, next to it, my father's ugly orange button-down, which he probably wore because it will never stain and because we always joke that it's impossible to do anything but laugh when you see him in it. My heart crumples a little knowing he probably wants me to laugh, even when I want to scream. I stand up, waving to them, trying to ignore the fingers pointing at me as Danny finally notices me and waves. He mimes something but I can't figure out what he means.

Only when the police officers begin to force people outside the room by closing the doors do I understand.

"Let's get the meeting started!" The school board chair bangs his gavel.

The meeting is going to begin. And my parents are trapped outside the doors. Danny can't muscle his way in even though I can tell he's trying all his tricks. But even the side door is blocked by Mrs. Himmelrath, who probably slept here to be the first in line. My parents were late only because they were pushing their way through the store protesters and stopping to talk to reporters, constantly showing their support for me.

Then I notice him.

Lucas is only a few feet away from me, close enough that I can see his knee bouncing the way it always does when he's anxious; his eyes dart left to right, and I realize he's looking anywhere but forward. Anywhere but at me.

It's impossible to feel more alone in a crowd than I do right now, even with a lawyer by my side.

"I'll begin by making some remarks—you do not have to speak if you would rather the meeting progress without your direct involvement," Mr. Wekstein says to me. Instead of finding someone I know, I now force myself to talk, this time to Mr. Wekstein, the ACLU lawyer who appeared in town as if sprinkled by unicorn dust. When he came to the house last night, he explained how the ACLU litigates and helps to educate communities about causes. "I'm a cause?" I'd asked as my mom handed out soy pigs in a blanket because it occurred to her that maybe he didn't eat pork. Mr. Wekstein held his food on a striped paper napkin but didn't eat. "It's our job to protect each individual's rights, Tessa. You have rights." It was easier to believe it in the safety of my house. Now it doesn't feel that way.

All last night while I tried to fall asleep I pictured this moment. The crowd (which is bigger than I imagined) and the murmurs (which are louder than I envisioned) die out and everyone focuses on me. Just one kid. Girl.

"I'm just a girl," I say into the microphone, my voice catching on the reverb, startling everyone into total quiet. "I'm just a girl who wants to go to a dance."

Last night, this was where I'd make the pretend crowd jump up and clap for me. It was easy in the half-dark of my bedroom to invoke the cinema-worthy drama—how rousing the cheers, how kind the smiles on everyone's faces.

"You're a girl who is corrupting this entire town!"

"Expel Tessa!"

This one catches on. "Expel Tessa! Expel Tessa!"

So much for the way I wanted things to go. I put the CD Josie gave me on repeat in my room, each song bleeding into the next, the words and music washing over me. My favorite one, albeit the most random, is some French punk song called "Ça Plane Pour Moi." My basic French skills are enough to let me pick out bits of the lyrics from the jumping, thrashing beat: "It works for me, it works for me." Maybe because nothing else is working for me at the moment. When I first met Josie, the thing that got us talking was music—how much of it she knows, how she quotes from songs all the time, mainly because I guess music was her comfort as she moved from town to town because of her mom's job as a professor. "You have to follow the employment," Josie had told me. "But music can be with you in any city or state."

I look around the room now, hearing the pulsing French song in my mind as though it alone tells me there's more to the world than this stifling meeting room. There's more to the world—my world—than the bitter faces and glances thrust my way tonight. It's hard to remember that. Almost impossible.

I picture being in my car, with Josie's CD blaring, the windows down, spring heat wafting in, and wish I could be there, driving away from here. Who is in the passenger seat? Josie, knowing all the lyrics? Or am I alone? Used to be, Lucas was the one next to me, our fingers fighting over the radio dial until we'd finally settle for some lame oldies station or Miss Kaboom. I feel the smallest of grins start to register on my mouth but still feel as though I am left to battle this one out myself.

Mr. Wekstein's white hair grows in wisps around his head but the top is bald and as shiny as the gymnasium floor. But he seems comfortable, like he knows what he's doing. Which makes one of us.

"Mr. Wekstein," I whisper now. He instinctively covers the microphone with his palm. "I think this is a lost cause."

As soon as the words are out I know it's true.

This town is small. It is closed. It is not New York City or Boston or San Francisco, where you can maybe turn out to like girls and not be shunned. Not find another brick smashed through your car window like I did this morning, with "get" on one side and "out" on the other. The tiny glass shards were scattered all over the dashboard and coated the passenger seat. That's what I have for company. Broken glass.

My feet bounce, nerves rocketing through me, and I chew on my lip, wishing I could be anywhere else.

That my simple plea would be heard.

That I could go to a dance with someone I like.

"Tessa Masterson has demanded this meeting," Mrs. Abernathy says.

I shake my head and grab Mr. Wekstein's gray suit-jacket sleeve. "That's totally not true," I seethe.

"We demand to be heard, too!" Mrs. Himmelrath shouts, waving her number in the air. "We will not stop until this town's values are restored!"

The entire room erupts in cheers and shouts, with faces I've known forever grimacing at me as I turn to look at the wall of people, the mass of bodies and feelings all swirling with hate and fear, and conviction that I am the single biggest issue ever.

Mr. Wekstein leans forward. "Tessa Masterson is challenging the school policy, which is directly in violation of her constitutional rights."

Only two people clap.

I am one of them.

16

LUKE

Here's what I'm thinking. I'm thinking about how Tessa always had my back in every single playground dispute in elementary school. Four square, tetherball, "Your mom fired my big sister from the Giant Brooks bakery"—whatever the fight was about, I always had Tessa on my side. This meant a lot, especially in the early years, because she was taller and, I can admit this now, tougher than me until at least the fifth grade. Well, she's still tougher than me, but I was talking about physically.

So as speaker after speaker gets up and drones on about immorality and family values and the homosexual agenda, I just remember Tessa on the playground. I remember when we were in the fourth grade and she stopped a bunch of our classmates from making fun of a second grader who had wet his pants.

"You say one more word to him and you'll all be singing soprano," Tessa barked at the bullies. Which was kind of funny because it was the fourth grade, so they really were singing soprano already, but we had heard that line in an action movie and Tessa thought it sounded cool. The bullies obviously didn't know what it meant either, because all they had to say was a couple of quiet "shut ups" as Tessa turned and put her arm around the kid—Stevie Allgier—and walked him to the nurse's office.

I saw the whole thing too, and I wanted to step in, but I was afraid for some reason. I didn't want those guys to turn their nastiness toward me. But Tessa just didn't care.

Stevie Allgier is in the back of the room. I don't know which side he's on today, but if everybody Tessa had ever been nice to took her side, then she'd be going to the Prom with no questions asked.

Another speaker gets up. It's old, white-haired Mrs. Thompson who worked at Hailer's Drugstore for years before it closed. "I don't think this girl is going to turn anybody gay. Let her dance, for Chrissake."

Some woman I don't even recognize stands up and yells, "Blasphemy!" at Mrs. Thompson, who promptly flips her the bird. The school board chair bangs his gavel and sheriff's deputies escort both women out of the meeting. I hear cheers from outside the doors as they emerge, but I don't know who they're for.

Another person gets up and starts talking about how things were different when she was young, and what's the world coming to, and values, and blah blah blah. It's pretty easy to zone out. I find myself thinking back to my first day of work at Giant Brooks when I was fourteen. I wasn't really big enough to unload the trucks yet, so I mostly swept, dusted, cleaned, and occasionally bagged when it got busy. I mopped the floor in the meat department, which is just exactly as disgusting as it sounds. I'm pretty sure Mom made sure I'd have to do that as a kind of test to see how serious I was about working. It was gross, but I did it without complaining, and I'd already been cleaning my share of the apartment to Mom's high standards for years, so the floor was spotless when I was done. My reward for doing a good job was to take out all the blood-stained butcher paper they'd gone through in the morning. This wasn't bad at all because all the blood was in a big plastic bag, and a big bag of crumpled-up paper is pretty light.

I headed out to the Dumpster where three other teenage bag boys were passing a joint around. I threw the bag into the Dumpster and one of them held the joint out toward me. I was kind of stunned, and before I could come up with a response that would get me out of smoking without getting me labeled as some kind of goody-goody mama's boy wuss, Tessa's dad appeared.

"Boys," he said. "Office. Now."

He marched us all through the back toward the office. Only two people saw us, so it probably took five minutes for the news to reach every employee rather than the usual two.

Three guys had finished their interrogations and had come out of the office. The first one was hanging his head. The second one was muttering under his breath. The third one was crying. I was glad that I wasn't going to be the first one to cry after getting fired. I hoped I was going to be able to convince Mom of my innocence.

It turned out I didn't have to. Tessa came storming up the back steps to the office and went barging right into her dad's office. "Daddy," she said. "How long have we known Luke?"

"His whole life, more or less," I heard her dad say.

"Do you think he'd do anything this stupid? This disrespectful? Is that the kid who's been at our house like a million times?"

"No, sweetie, but this may come as a surprise to you—people sometimes do dumb things when they're teenagers."

"Well, not Luke. I can tell you right now what happened. He left the meat department with a bag of trash about ten seconds before you went out there. So how did he have time to get high?"

"Honey. I didn't say he was getting high, but I have to at least ask him what happened."

"You do not. You should trust him more than that."

Tessa lost that argument. I did have to go into Mr. Masterson's office and face him across his desk, which at that moment looked about five times bigger than it had ever looked before. And he did call Jim from the meat department up to verify my story, which infuriated Tessa. She fully believed that my word should be sacred because I was the same person they had always known.

And now, at last, it's my turn to speak. I suddenly realize how hot it is in here, as I approach the microphone. I can feel everybody looking at me as I unfold my little speech. "Ladies and gentlemen of the school board," I say, "I have known Tessa Masterson my entire life."

"Son, you get two minutes like everybody else," the board chair says, and everybody laughs at me. And this pisses me off enough that I just drop my speech.

"Well, it's not enough. Two minutes is not enough to sum up who Tessa is. While all kinds of people talked about values, I've been sitting here thinking about what a kind and loyal person she is. Aren't those values too? Aren't they important? And if they are, then why the hell aren't more people in this town living up to them? I know damn well I'm not the only person in this room who has received kindness and loyalty from Tessa or her parents or her brother. And now what? Now we all know a little bit more about who Tessa really is than we did before, and kindness and loyalty are out the window. I guess those values don't matter very much to people around here. Well, they should. Tessa Masterson and her whole family live those values every day. And charity? Is that a value? I don't have enough time to call out the names of every single person who's gotten a break from them when times were tough. But I'll tell you this: I've seen some of them in the Giant Brooks parking lot carrying signs telling people not to shop there. Some of them are in this room now. I don't know how you sleep at night. Tessa is the same kind, loyal, charitable person she's always been. She's not different. We're different. We're worse than we used to be. And we should be ashamed of ourselves. All of us."

That's all I can get out. I've seen enough movies that I kind of expect a slow clap at this point. I thought everybody would recognize how right I am, how stupid we've all been, and the whole thing would just blow over in a storm of applause.

Yeah, I'm stupid.

I turn from the mic and look at Tessa, but she's talking with her lawyer.

I sit down and wait through the rest of the speakers. They continue to run about four to one against Tessa. Finally the time expires and the school board chairman takes the mic. "Ladies and gentlemen, I believe one of our own students at Brookfield-Mason Regional High said it best: 'Our whole Prom is going to be about her instead of just being a normal dance. You don't have to rub everybody's nose in it and make people uncomfortable. Maybe some people won't even get to go to Prom now because of their religion.' Now it's the responsibility of the school board to consider the rights and interests of all of our students and families, not just one. We now ask everyone to clear the room so that the board can meet in executive session"—Tessa's ACLU lawyer pops out of his seat, and the board chair continues—"which is permitted under Indiana's open-meeting law, provided no votes are taken during the closed session. Following the executive session, the board will hold a vote. Thank you."

It takes five minutes for everyone to file out of the room. I try to catch Tessa's eye, but I can't see her in the crowd. I see Mom and think about trying to squeeze my way through the sea of bodies to go talk to her, but I'm afraid if I do that, I'll wind up talking to her and then I'll wind up crying. My big moment turned out to be spectacularly useless. My speech didn't fire up the sensible people that Kate Sweeney insists live in this town. And then they used my own words against me. I just feel like I'm never going to be able to make this right, and if I open my mouth to say anything to Mom, the whole thing is going to come pouring out of me in big sobs, and that is not something I want to do in front of the whole town.

So I stand and wait with everybody else. I have no idea what an executive session is or how long it lasts, and apparently nobody else does either. But after a half hour, people start grumbling about how they have things to do, and a handful leave. After an hour, about half the people in the room have left. And by the time two incredibly boring hours have passed, there are only sixteen of us still waiting.

The school board chair throws open the doors and announces that the board is ready for its vote.

After we've all gotten inside and taken our seats—Tessa

still won't look at me—the board chair calls the meeting to order again.

"We have reviewed everyone's testimony as well as the *very helpful* document presented to us by our *friend* from the *ACLU*. It is not a good use of the district's money to fight nuisance lawsuits, and it's not in the best interest of the students or the district to have what should be a wholesome student event transformed into a media circus."

I wonder what planet this guy lives on, because if he lives anywhere near Brookfield, he knows damn well that the Prom is an event where teachers and administrators famously look the other way while drunken students grope each other on the dance floor before piling into cars to go to some after party where they can drink even more and hope they can manage to have sex before they vomit.

"We will therefore vote on the motion to cancel this year's Prom. All in favor?" Nine of the eleven people on the board raise their hands and say "Aye."

"Opposed?" One person raises her hand. "Abstentions?" Another raises his.

"With the vote nine in favor, one opposed, and one abstention, this board hereby votes to cancel this year's Prom. This meeting is adjourned."

The board members start standing up and shuffling papers, and those of us in the audience stare at them like we can't believe they just did that. This is probably because we can't believe they just did that. You don't cancel Prom. Ever. The town still talks about the big floods in 1997, when the gym and most of the halls within about twenty miles of here were under water in March and not ready for dancing by May. They held Prom on the roof of the school under a tent that year. Nothing stops Prom. Ever. Until now.

Mom stands up, her face beet red. "You've just painted a target on this girl's back! Shame on you! Shame!"

The no and the abstention actually do look ashamed, but the rest of the board hold their heads high as they leave.

I wish I could do the same, but somehow I can't bring my gaze above my shoes as I head to the back of the room. Mom tries to put her arm around my shoulders, but I've been taller than her for three years, so it doesn't really work. "Come on, kid," she says. "Let's go home. It stinks in here."

Outside, there is no crowd of sensible people ready to put me on their shoulders and carry me home. There are also no lunatics with signs screaming at us. It's just another quiet night in Brookfield, except they've just turned Tessa from an interesting freak show into the most hated person in town. And I still feel like it's my fault.

17

><

Tessa

For about thirty seconds, Lucas was my boyfriend. It was summer, two years ago, the tail end of it, when people spend their mornings buying binders and new jeans but then wind up meeting at the lake to soak up every bit of sun and water, flirting as much as they can before being herded back to the linoleum and poster-lined classrooms.

I had worked a double shift, cleaning out the entire freezer section so we could make way for a new, supposedly greener unit that would leave less of a carbon footprint while prominently displaying the squeezy tubes of iced raspberry lemonade. I was tired but tan, and my hair had gone all coppery white at the front, so maybe I looked pretty. A group of us from the cross-country team had planned to meet for a casual lake swim but somehow while I'd been sticking my hands into the permafrost, my fingers aching and red, our outing had become an opportunity to dress up and drink.

As a result, I showed up at the lake but was redirected to the yacht club. Lake Markunmakee is the only large body of water for hours, and from May to September is populated by the wealthiest kids from Indianapolis and Chicago, who summer at their enormous houses and dock their boats at the club.

"Looks like it's just you and me," Lucas had said when we'd parked by the communal beach. The sand was poorly kept, with razor-sharp clamshells making it hazardous to walk barefoot. As we padded along the waterline, toddlers in their soggy diapers plopped in the sand, fussing while their local parents looked bored and annoyed.

"We could just get a root beer float," I said, and Lucas and I were halfway to the Shake Shack before a blue Mini Cooper convertible swerved up and stopped short. Lucas raised his eyebrows at me.

"Hey there, hot one," said the driver. I squinted and realized he was the tall, blond guy who had come into Giant Brooks while I was working and made some joke about squeeze pops being his main squeeze or something lame like that.

"Did he seriously just call you that?" Lucas's words came out tense. I put my hand on his arm to keep him from saying something that would inspire a summer fight. With only boats, tubing, and beer for kicks, fights were common. Very masculine.

"Hey," I said brightly, shielding my eyes from the hazy sun. "We're just getting a float."

"No you're not—you're coming with us." He smiled and motioned for us to hop in the backseat. "Your teammates sent me to collect you." He looked directly at me to make the point that he was getting me, not Lucas.

"Where are we going?" I asked, with the emphasis on "we" so he'd get that Lucas was part of the package.

"Yacht club formal!"

My face must've fallen, because the blond guy immediately shook his head and pushed his body partway out of the driver's seat so he could face us. "Just kidding. It's a luau. You know, pig on a spit, pineapple . . . grass skirts."

"I like a grass skirt," Lucas said, and I thwacked his arm.

When we got to the club, the sun was half slung into the lake, and ripples of pink and yellow appeared on the wide porch where people were dancing, eating from china plates, and looking like they'd spent more on their grass-skirt-and-bikini-top ensembles than Lucas's mom did on her rent. Lucas went right for a big plate of grub and I stood there, feeling totally underdressed in my flip-flop and shorts, thankful I'd at least shoved a clean shirt in my bag.

"Want to dance?" the blond guy, whose name I still didn't know, asked. I shrugged. That's how I was feeling back then—like, um, not really, but if you really want to, I will. Like it was expected of me so often I just went along with it, shrugging over questions about which boy

I liked, about Valentine's Day crushes, about dates I didn't go on.

So I shrugged my way onto the dance floor, my worn-in flip-flops tracking sand onto the high-gloss wood. All around me, Hawaiian-print sarongs and string-bikini tops pressed themselves to boys with summer-ripped chests, bright polo shirts. The blond guy held me first at arm's length. Then, as the song shifted to something slower, closer, his hands moved down onto my waist. I closed my eyes, trying to pretend I was somewhere else. With someone else. Then his grip tightened and his fingers began to roam, making what I'm sure he thought were slow, sexy circles on my shouder blades and then trying to creep toward the front.

"Um, those are my breasts," I said because I couldn't think of any clever way to get my point across.

Blond guy grinned and whispered into my ear. "Yes, they are!"

I have decent boobs. I know that. I have to special-order good running bras. This does not mean that I wanted some summer boy attempting the creep-and-crawl to feel them.

So I pushed away.

And he pulled back.

It was like a less fun version of row, row, row your boat, only by the time I'd pulled back yet again, the guy was getting annoyed, and his friends and my slightly ine-briated teammates clearly thought we were meant to be hooking up on the dance floor because they were not helping me.

And then came Lucas to my rescue.

"Hi, Sweetie," he said. He didn't grab me or rudely push this guy aside in some overly manly show of strength. He just stood there, calm, on the dance floor, and knew exactly what to do. He tilted his head, looked at me—at the two of us—in such a deep way that the blond guy stopped swaying and wrestling with me.

"Hi," I said, not knowing what would happen next.

He turned to the blond guy. Oh God, I'd thought, here's where things get ugly. Punches would be thrown. Stitches sewn into eyebrows, noses broken.

But no. Lucas sighed as though he had nowhere he had to be, nothing to do except finish eating his pineapple-encrusted pork barbecue. "Thank you kindly for watching over Sweetie—I call her Sweetie, see, because we're betrothed—you know, meant to be together." I fought laughter but the blond guy and everyone around us listened seriously. "I have a blood-sugar condition that requires me to eat every two point two hours, but I'm finished now." He wiped his mouth on the napkin and then held his plate out for the blond guy. "If you wouldn't mind throwing this out for me while Sweetie and I enjoy one last dance?" Lucas never broke from his stance— only I knew he was bs-ing his way through everything— and the guy actually accepted the dirty plate and balled-up, sauce-covered napkin as Lucas stepped closer to me.

I didn't want Lucas to gloat later—he loves a good gloat—so I added my two cents. "See, Lucas and I, we're—"

"Boyfriend and girlfriend?" the blond guy questioned, disappointment on his face.

"Oh, more than that," I said. "We're saving ourselves for marriage! For each other!"

I thought I'd done well. That I'd one-upped the conversation.

And for about thirty seconds, we were a couple, with Lucas's hands on my waist, mine linked over his shoulders. It felt good. Safe. Both of us laughed under our breath.

"So you're, like, virgins together?" The blond guy stood with Lucas's plate in his hands.

I blushed. Lucas looked like he'd swung hard and missed big-time.

"We're . . . you know, we're . . . ," I started to say, but by the time Lucas got around to saying, "We're as pure as baby unicorns on freshly fallen angel snow," the guy and his friends had dissolved into a swell of laughter.

Lucas and I left, and walked the three miles back to the Shake Shack and split battered onion rings and a large root-beer float.

"So, you like it when I come to your rescue?" He'd elbowed me as the mosquitoes dove for my bare ankles. "Did I save you or what?"

— — — — —

As I leave the school board meeting, the faces of the board members convey what I already know. They won. I lost. Was there even a fair fight?

"This isn't over, Tessa," Mr. Wekstein says, and goes off to find my parents.

I'm caught in the wave of bodies edging for the door. There aren't many of us now, but we get clumped together on the steps that lead to the parking lot. I notice Lucas's sneakers before I see his face. His Nikes were a point of contention with his mom, who insists that brand names are for suckers and that when he was young, Zips were just fine. I stood up for Lucas on that one, saying how all the real athletes had good shoes, how important it is to feel like one of the team. Now of course, I'm not really part of any team. I look up and see Lucas, remembering how at the yacht club he'd delivered his speech with barbecue sauce on his upper lip, how he'd wanted to be my savior, how I'd wanted it, too. I swallow as I recall the words he said tonight. How they seemed so small. Yes, he tried and for that I give him a nod. But that's all. His voice wasn't powerful enough, he wasn't able to cut in and protect me, and now he isn't able to even make me forget about my worries with vanilla ice cream and sweet soda.

Last year, when we sat on the picnic table swatting at the bugs and finishing the onion rings, Lucas had slung his arm across my shoulder and said, "Was I great back there or what?"

"The best," I said, overly loud, and let my head drop onto him.

"Right back at ya," he said, and slurped the last bit from the waxy root beer float.

— — — — — —

Now, in the parking lot, our eyes meet, and I say, "Um, thanks." And those words, too, are small in the big night air. We stand there for just a second. Then we walk to our separate cars and drive out different exits.

18

LUKE

I go home after the board meeting and crawl into bed. Saturday morning I'm up early for my shift at the supermarket. The crowd outside is bigger and angrier than before. The good news is that people holding pro-Tessa, pro–Giant Brooks signs are out in force too. They're still outnumbered, but they're here.

The anti-Tessa protesters yell at me as I walk into work. Stuff about God, stuff about Prom, stuff about evil. I know I shouldn't do it, but I stop and try to talk to one. "Do you think it might be evil to try to throw people out of work in a town where not too many people have jobs?" I ask a woman with a sign that says STAND AGAINST EVIL.

"Christ threw the money changers out of the temple," she replies. "I suppose you'd have wanted him to protect their precious jobs."

"I don't know what you're talking about," I say.

"Well if you learned your scripture, you might understand something about right and wrong," she says. "Your ignorance of the Word just shows why we need prayer in schools!"

"Lady, I don't need to read the Bible to know that it's wrong to hate people. If you think your religion is telling you to come to our town and stir up hate, then either you or your religion or both are really stupid."

This actually manages to shut her up. I walk away while she's still making gasping fish faces and head into the store.

Business has been slow here lately, but it's dead today. Saturday. Which is bad. Unless there's a basketball game, people around here do their shopping on Saturday and their churching on Sunday. A few people wander the aisles buying stuff, but for the most part the place is eerily quiet.

I see Tessa's dad walking through the store. He looks worried. I guess when your business depends on making money from stuff that tends to go bad quickly, a few days like this one can pretty much wreck you.

On break time, I buy a bag of pretzels and an energy drink at the front and take them back into the break room, where Josie is sitting alone at the table.

"Hey," she says. She's eating a sandwich and doesn't really look at me.

"Hey," I say. I can barely look at her, I'm so ashamed. I'm trying to think of a way to get out of here, but since I obviously came back here for my break, I can't just turn around and leave. I'm the one who created the awkwardness, so I'm gonna have to deal with it. I sit at the table across from Josie.

I open my bag of sourdough pretzels. It's pretty noisy, and Josie gives me an annoyed look. "Pretzel?" I say. "Makes a nice accompaniment to a sandwich."

"Bad carbs," Josie says. "I'm only eating whole grains right now."

I pause at that for a minute. "Guess that's why your sandwich roll is so brown."

Josie looks at me like I'm stupid. "Yep. Whole wheat."

"So, uh, do they make whole-wheat pretzels?" This is horrible. When I got braces in the eighth grade, they had to take a couple of my teeth out. That sucked way less than this conversation.

Josie gives me the are-you-stupid-or-what? stare again, then looks back at her sandwich. "Look," she says, "you were Tessa's best friend for years. There must be a reason for that, so I figure I should try not to hate you, just out of respect for her. You know?"

"Um. I guess."

"But it is a daily struggle for me not to punch you in your stupid face."

"Yeah. I pretty much want to punch myself in my stupid face most of the time these days. But I'm too pretty to mess up my face, so I usually just go for the ribs. Hurts like hell but doesn't leave any marks."

Josie stares at me again.

"That was a joke," I said. "I don't really punch myself. I just have to kind of live with the guilt."

"Tessa said you spoke up for her at the meeting," Josie says, wiping the corner of her mouth with a napkin. I'm actually kind of excited to hear that Tessa thought enough of my lame speech to mention it to Josie.

"Yeah. I did."

"She said it was nice, but ineffectual." And there goes the excitement.

"Right again."

"So what else are you going to do?" She takes a big bite of her sandwich.

"I-I don't know. I mean, it looks like we're beaten. I guess I thought I would try to stop anybody who was trying to beat her up at school."

Josie smiles. "So you could get that punch in the face you've been craving?"

I laugh. "Maybe."

Josie folds up the deli paper that had held her sandwich and stands up. "Tessa told me about how you got that creep to leave her alone at a dance one time."

That story. I'm surprised she mentioned it to Josie. Hopefully she didn't mention how awkward my dancing was, since I was trying to both slow dance and disguise the fact that I had a boner from dancing with a girl who was supposedly just a friend but was still, you know, a girl.

"Yeah."

"At one point in your life, you knew how to do the right thing, and that it wasn't about fighting. So figure something out. Or don't. I don't really care. But I guess I kind of wish you would. 'Cause you still mean a lot to Tessa, and I'd rather not hate you. So maybe you can make it easier for me." She throws her paper away and heads for the door. "I left the mustard. You shouldn't eat pretzels without mustard," she says. "Just bring it back to the deli when you're done."

"Thanks," I say, but she's already out the door.

I spend the rest of my shift thinking, and I only come up with one thing. So when I get off work at four, I swing by the library and get there at four fifteen. "We close at four thirty," the librarian says.

"Thanks," I say. "I'll only be a minute."

I log on to Facebook and go to the "100,000 Strong for Tessa Masterson" page, which has suddenly got 12,076 members. I wonder if the school board meeting made the national news or something. I post this:

Hey everybody. If you care about this at all, please come to Brookfield and buy some groceries at Giant Brookfield Market. Tessa's parents own it, and it may close due to boycotts and protests. Thank you.

I start "liking" pretty much every gay and lesbian page I can find and posting a version of my message on every one. I guess this will make my Facebook profile look pretty gay: Lucas Fogelman likes "Gay Hoosiers," "Valpo GSA," "Lesbian Avengers" (that one sounds kinda scary, but what the hell), "Out and Proud in the Midwest"—well, you get the idea. I wonder what my future teammates at Purdue will make of this. I imagine it might make for some locker-room awkwardness. And I don't care. At least, I try really really hard not to care. I guess that's a step.

After my thrilling Saturday night with the Xbox, Mom wakes me up early. Well, okay, it's ten thirty, but I was killing zombies until three, so it feels early to me. "Come on, kid, we gotta go."

"What? Are we like suddenly going to church or something?"

"You wish. No, the Shillito's in the mall is going out of business."

"I guess I'm still not clear what makes this a wake-Luke-up-at-the-crack-of-dawn-on-Sunday-morning-situation."

"First of all, dawn cracked about five hours ago. Second of all, they open at eleven, and you may not have noticed that we haven't had new sheets or towels in four years, but I certainly have. Linens are very expensive, and this is our chance to get some dirt cheap."

"See, again, I'm kind of confused about why this needs to involve me."

Mom sighs and wipes her brow with the back of her hand. "Because I want your company, okay? You had to force me to say it?"

"Uh. Lemme get showered and dressed."

"Ten minutes."

"Okay."

Shillito's is packed with bargain shoppers. They're mostly Mom's age and older. It's hard to move through the aisles and displays, and twice somebody throws an elbow at me when I'm reaching for a sheet set.

Mom watches this with amusement, and then annoyance. "Okay, go wander the mall—you're clearly not cut out for this."

I wander the rest of the mall. It's kind of a sad place, though not as sad as the street where I live. But MegaMart has done its share of damage here too. About a third of the storefronts are covered over with painted wood and signs that say COMING SOON! ANOTHER GREAT BUSINESS FOR MASON MALL CUSTOMERS!

I look around at GameStop but don't see anything I like enough to pay for. I see plenty of things I like in the window of Victoria's Secret, but I don't really have anyone to buy them for, and I'm pretty sure that's a creepy gift anyway. I come to Wild Thingz! and look through the window at all the black T-shirts. It's not my kind of store.

Or, I didn't think it was my kind of store. But there's Kate Sweeney behind the register, looking bored. So I wander in. Just to be friendly.

"You're not nearly pale enough to work here," I say.

Kate laughs. "Yeah, well, you're not nearly pale enough to shop here," she says. "I'm trying to keep boredom at

bay, or, at least, you know, be bored somewhere besides my house. What's your excuse?"

"Mom's buying sheets at Shillito's, and I think if I got injured by a bargain shopper, the scholarship people at Purdue might be a little pissed. After they stopped laughing at me."

Kate laughs, which is actually pretty thrilling. "So what are you in the market for here?" she asks. "T-shirt? How about this one?" She points to one that says I ♥ THE DIFFERENTLY BIOTIC.

"Um," I say.

"Or one of these?" she says, pointing to two that say TEAM JOSHUA and TEAM GREGORY.

"What the hell are those about?"

"*Crimson Sunset?*"

"Oh my God. Is that that vampire thing that all the freshman girls were into two years ago?"

"Yeah. We still move a fair amount of the T-shirts. And it's not just vampire stuff. Joshua's the werewolf."

"I mean, so people actually buy these shirts about whether they like the imaginary werewolf or the imaginary vampire and they, like, wear them around?"

"Oh my God, yeah. We had an actual girl fight in here over that very important issue. Two girls started yelling and before long it came to slapping and scratching."

"Hot!" I say, laughing. "I mean, what the hell goes on in a girl's mind that makes her want to do that?"

Kate smiles. "What goes on in a guy's mind, like, ever?"

"Well, you're looking at the guy who fell in love with a lesbian, so I guess I can say guys are pretty damn stupid. At least I am."

"Good thing you're cute, then."

Once again I find myself kind of tongue-tied. I mean, I'm dumb enough to have fallen in love with a lesbian, but I know when I'm being flirted with. What I don't know is what the hell to do about it. I used to, but that was back when I thought I knew who Tessa was, and who I was, and both of those things turned out to be wrong, so my confidence is kind of in the toilet right now. My eyes are darting around the store looking for something else to pay attention to, because the operating system in my brain is going to crash if I keep thinking about the fact that a really cute college girl is flirting with me.

And I see the T-shirt press and the sign that says CUSTOM SHIRTS MADE HERE, and my brain, eager to do something right, makes a connection.

"Hey," I say. "Can you, um, I mean, thank you, by the way, but, I mean, uh, can you make me a T-shirt?"

Kate laughs at me, but her eyes are kind of twinkly, so it's okay. I think. "You are a smooth operator! Can you make me a T-shirt! What girl could resist that line?"

I'm blushing, and I hate that. "Well, yeah. I told you I was an idiot."

"Well, every guy is. At least you can admit it. And yeah, I can make you a T-shirt. It's what they pay me to do. What do you want on it?"

I tell her, and she smiles. "Okay, that is adorable."

She makes me the T-shirt, and I meet Mom at the fountain, which isn't turned on and therefore looks gross and sad. Mom, however, holds several huge white plastic bags and is beaming.

"I just can't tell you what new soft towels and new sheets are going to do for my quality of life," Mom says.

"Congrats," I say.

"What'd you get?" Mom asks, and I show her my T-shirt.

"Are they actually selling those?" Mom says.

"I had it made," I say.

"I am totally getting one," Mom says. It occurs to me to beg Mom to stop, to tell her that her walking into Wild Thingz! and getting a T-shirt from Kate Sweeney is going to embarrass the hell out of me in front of an attractive young woman, but maybe it's just time for me to grow up.

I don't, however, grow up enough to go in the store with her. Ten minutes later, Mom comes out with her own shirt.

"That girl likes you," Mom says as we're driving home.

"Yeah," I say. "Well. I don't know. Yeah, she flirts with me and stuff, but she's in college. Plus, you know—"

"Grow a pair and ask her out, will you?"

I sigh. "Mom. This is probably going to sound really weird and you're probably going to make fun of me, but as much as, wow, I would love to go out with an adorable college girl, I just feel like this—I'm going to be spending a lot of time trying to redeem myself over the next month, and I . . . I owe Tessa a lot, and I don't want to be distracted from that project, and I'm afraid any girl would just be, like, jealous, you know—why are you spending all this time on Tessa?—and I just think I shouldn't go out with anybody until this thing is kind of settled or whatever. You know?"

Mom doesn't answer, but I see her starting to well up. "Quit making me so damn proud of you when I have to drive," she says.

Just then my phone buzzes, and despite the fact that we haven't exchanged numbers, I have this irrational hope that it's a text from Kate. Only it isn't from Kate.

"This is Josie," it says. "You should change your Facebook privacy settings." I don't know what that means. "Anyone can get your #. Just wanted to say that this is the kind of thing I meant and I hate you less now."

I look at my phone, perplexed, and send this back: "What thing?"

I get this ten seconds later: "Giant Brooks."

"Hey Mom," I say, "can we swing by Giant Brooks on the way home?"

Mom says okay, and when we drive by, we see this: the parking lot is full of cars. Okay, not full. Probably two-thirds full. But yesterday it was three-quarters empty, so it's a big improvement. Who knows if it's enough to save anybody's job. But it's something.

Monday morning comes, and, heart pounding, I ready myself for another attempt to make things right. At seven thirty, I walk into school wearing my new T-shirt. It says TEAM TESSA.

19

Tessa

I should have taken up fencing instead of running. The mask, the white protective gear, it would come in handy right about now. But of course our school doesn't have fencing—we barely have track and all that requires is a surface on which to run—because the district can't afford the gear and the parents can't scrape together extra funds like they do for a new football mascot. Actually, the football mascot outfit—a misshapen beaver—would be great now, too, although it wouldn't do much for the ridicule factor.

But I have nothing to protect me. Nothing to hide behind as I drive into the parking lot and realize that what I first thought was spring hail is actually a shower of candy. Not in a Willy Wonka way of "Wouldn't it be so awesome if it rained gumdrops," more like someone raided the MegaMart of all its stale Easter candy and is now chucking it from the second-floor roof. I turn my windshield wipers on to deflect the jujubes and rejected black jelly beans and carefully roll down my window so I can look up: mistake number one because as I stick my head out, the group of kids on the roof hurls fistfuls of suckers at me. A mint wrapped in green cellophane hits my forehead and slides into the collar of my shirt and I duck back inside the relative safety of my car.

For the first five months of senior year Lucas and I carpooled. Well, not carpooled, exactly, because he never drove. For all his hand-eye coordination on the field he's not the best driver, not to mention most of the time he can't afford to fix his car, so I would pick him up. The first couple of mornings he was waiting for me early, leaning on the window ledge outside the boarded-up drugstore below his apartment. He was so happy to see me, so happy that it was still warm and we had an extra twenty minutes before the first bell to just hang out together. I shove my books into my bag and inhale sharply to fortify myself. I wince—not just at the long walk from the parking lot to the school's double doors, but because I remember that first morning when I picked up Lucas. He'd brought homemade Arnold Palmers—half lemonade, half iced tea. I'd brought leftover pecan rolls from the pastry platter my parents had lugged home. Then every morning after that, we shared breakfast.

Now I am alone. My stomach rumbles because I didn't bring breakfast with me, and Lucas didn't slip into the passenger seat with a cold travel mug thoughtfully wrapped with a paper napkin. I undo my seat belt, sling my bag over my shoulder, and exit the car like it's any other day. If I can pretend it's normal, maybe it will be normal.

"Screw you, Masterson!" Marcus Denner and a group of his thuggy football players make a threatening huddle near Marcus's F-150. When Marcus first got his license Danny and Lucas and a few of my fellow runners piled in the back of the pickup and rode around for hours, just beeping the horn and laughing, sharing bags of BBQ chips from my parents' store.

"Way to ruin everything." Marcus's girlfriend, Tina, steps out in front of me and for a second I think she's going to shove me—and maybe she thinks about it, but then realizes she's built like a sapling and I could deck her easily.

I keep walking, and a shower of sweets stings my skin as gumdrops land on my shoulders, caramel squares peck my head. Who knew candy could leave marks?

I walk faster, but I don't run because I fear if I do, I will start bawling or turn back. Plus Marcus and his buddies and Tina's crew of girls—who will never leave this town, staying to work at the MegaMart or Supercuts and talking of high school as the best time ever—keep following me in a swarm.

Inside, it's no better.

My locker is slimed with shaving cream and what appears to be honey mixed with red food coloring, giving it the look of oozing blood.

"I can't believe this," I say aloud. Determined not to give up, I march to the principal's office and go right up to the desk. "My locker has been vandalized again."

"And?" So much for massive concern from the secretary.

"And my essay for American Lit is in there," I say.

"Well, reprint it."

"But it's due today. Now." I feel the anger, the frustration threatening to form tears.

"I'm afraid I can't help you."

I look at her, and look over my shoulder at the kids in the hall, all of them stone-faced.

"Forget it," I say. "I'll just figure it out myself."

Before the bell rings, Jenny Himmelrath approaches my locker, where I am trying in vain to scoop up the glop with cheap paper towels from the janitor's closet. He wouldn't even help me when I asked; he just shook his head and muttered under his breath that I'm the girl who ruined the whole Prom for everyone. "Just so you know," Jenny says, "I'm not totally horrified about you . . . your . . . um, sexuality."

Wow. So not what I expected from her. I begin to crack a smile but she keeps talking. "But it's like, keep it to yourself, you know? You're rubbing it in everyone's face with this whole bring-a-girl-to-Prom thing and now look what you've done." Her volume increases. "I special-ordered a dress I can't wear and all my plans—everyone's plans—are screwed up because of you." I stare at her. I could say that me bringing Josie to the Prom is no more rubbing anything in anyone's faces than her bringing a guy. I could say she can wear the dress another time.

But instead, what ends up coming out is, "I'm sorry, okay? I didn't know it would be like this." She stares at me and everyone around us is quiet. A few sneakers squeak on the linoleum, someone closes a locker.

"But it *is* like this. And it's all your fault."

Jenny glares and walks away. I stand there as people head off to Trig and Chemistry and American Lit with papers that aren't trapped in their disgusting lockers, and I sink down to the floor, still clutching the honey-sticky paper towels. Then I bolt to the bathroom.

I stay there through first and second periods, debating whether to go home or not, then imagining the humiliation I'd feel. But it's stupid being in the bathroom anyway. I'm about to emerge from the stall when I hear voices and, like a field mouse, I dart back in and lock the stall door.

"Anyway," the voice says, "Jenny says her mom has a plan."

"Serves her right," another voice says.

I peer through the crack and try to see who the voices belong to, but all I see is a hot-pink tank top and fake-tanned legs, which could be any number of girls.

"They say her lawyer is gay. It's like a club."

"Well, if Jenny says there's a plan, you know there is. Hey, give me your gloss, okay?"

And with that, they leave, the door whispering shut behind them.

What plan does Mrs. Himmelrath have? An anti-me parade through town, complete with homophobic floats? I stare at my blotchy face in the mirror. I will clean my locker and then go home. That's my own plan. I grab a fistful of paper towels, dampen them, and head out to the crowded corridor.

Stares. Glares. Someone spits on my shoe and I'm wearing flip-flops so it's super-gross, but I don't flinch. The ACLU lawyer told me to expect this, but thinking about it and experiencing it are very different things. He plans on filing a suit against the school board, but it isn't easy. And each step he takes toward "helping my cause" makes me feel less and less a part of this town. This school. Less a part of anywhere. "Look," Mr. Wekstein had said on speakerphone with my parents and me last night, "they're going to blame you for everything— ruining the Prom, the town, anything they can think of." And they do.

"Who did it?" Danny asks when he finds me heading to my locker.

"Who cares?" I say, and hand him paper towels. "Just help me get it off before I drive home."

He grabs my shoulder and looks at me too close. "No. You can't leave. You can't let the other team—"

"No sports pep talks, okay?" I keep walking to my locker, trying to figure out the best way to de-scum it, but when I get there, it is honey-free, no shaving cream, no slurs. Just clean and dry.

Danny looks surprised. "Guess maintenance finally caved," he says.

I look down the corridor and see no one. Everyone's gone to class. Then I turn and look the other way, past the principal's office toward the front entrance and there's the answer.

It's Lucas, one hand clutching a spray bottle of some kind, the other holding a balled-up Brookfield-Mason baseball shirt—the blue-trimmed one only MVPs get. We lock eyes right before he chucks the shirt in the trash, pausing for a second, maybe waiting for me to shout something to him. Then he rounds the corner toward the gym.

Danny gives my hand a squeeze before bolting to class; he's late already and they'll probably give him detention just because he's related to me. I should go to class, too, but I don't. I open my locker, find my essay, walk it to my American Lit room, and hand it to Mr. Nichols while everyone watches me, waiting for me to take my seat.

But I don't sit in class. I pivot and leave. Walking past my now-clean locker, I reach into my pocket and pull out one of the mints that had hit me in the face and pop it in my mouth. I'm halfway out the door when I stop. The trash can is giant and smells like old fries and sweat, but I reach in and retrieve Lucas's shirt. It would be a shame to throw away something that meant so much.

20

><

LUKE

Wearing my TEAM TESSA shirt to school turns out to be way less interesting to my fellow students than I had hoped. Everybody who might have been offended by it already hated me for not hating Tessa as thoroughly as they thought their religion demanded. I did have one girl I didn't know—a short, chubby ninth grader with that weird orangey colored hair that I guess comes from bleaching hair that's too dark to go blond or something—ask me where I got the shirt. "Wild Thingz!" I say. "But, I mean, they made it for me."

"Cool," she says, and flees down the hallway.

Of course Tessa's locker has been vandalized, since she's now the Evil Lesbian Who Canceled Prom. The fact that the school board actually canceled Prom is true and logical, but truth and logic don't seem to be very popular around here these days.

So I clean it. It's not that big a deal, but I figure it's the least I can do. And yeah, I could go into the bathroom and get lots of paper towels and clean it up, but, with our last baseball game behind us, I kind of feel like using my Brookfield-Mason jersey. I'll be wearing a Boilermakers jersey soon enough, and I can't imagine I'll want to put on a jersey that represents this school ever again in my life.

Also, I threw a shutout when I wore it early in the season, and after that I figured it would probably be bad luck to wash it. Which probably qualifies it as toxic waste at this point. So I wipe all the goo off Tessa's locker with my reeking jersey and some cleaning spray I took from the custodian's cart, which was abandoned in the hallway with no custodian in sight.

Then I throw my jersey into the trash. And it feels kind of good.

Walking down the hall toward my first class, I get stopped by Mr. Stroudt, the assistant principal. "Luke, can you step into my office, please?" he says.

"Okay," I say.

"Have a seat," he says, gesturing at the chair in front of the desk. So it's one of those conversations. I plant myself in a hard plastic chair in front of his desk, and he walks around to the back and sits down in his comfortable chair. "Now, Luke, are you familiar with the student handbook?"

I really want to tell him that of course I've memorized the student handbook—doesn't everyone?—but I decide to just play it cool. "I know the rules," I say.

"Well, son, I'm afraid maybe you don't. Here," he says, reaching onto a bookshelf behind his desk and tossing me a copy of the student handbook. "Will you open this to page thirty-seven please?"

"Uh. Okay," I say.

"Will you read the section entitled 'Dress Code'?"

"Sure," I say. I start reading it to myself, though I know where this is going.

"Read it aloud, please," Mr. Stroudt says.

Maybe it's senioritis. Maybe it's that I just spent ten minutes cleaning gross goo off a locker and knowing that the dildo or dildos who did it are not getting punished. But I'm not reading the dress code aloud.

"I can read it," I say.

"I know you can. Now read it aloud, please."

There's a pause. I hear my mom's voice in my head, telling me never to mouth off to cops or bosses or anybody that can make your life hell. "Swallow your pride and don't go to jail," she said.

I try for middle ground. Why haven't I figured out yet that there's no middle ground here anymore?

"Sir, I can read the passage. I would prefer not to read it aloud."

And Stroudt's face is suddenly pink. He's out of his chair and yelling. "Did I ask you what you preferred?" he bellows. "Do you recall me asking whether you preferred to read aloud?"

I don't say anything.

"Answer my question! Did I ask you what you preferred?"

"Sir, I don't believe that's a serious question. If you have a real question for me, I'll be happy to answer it."

He looks like his head might explode with rage. "Okay, mister! You want a real question? Here's a real question for you! Why do you think you're getting suspended from school today?"

"I couldn't say, sir. Though since you had me read the dress code section, I have to assume it's because I'm wearing a halter top, belly shirt, or short shorts."

I am, in fact, wearing my TEAM TESSA shirt, jeans, and a ratty pair of sneakers I've had for a year.

"Very funny. If you had bothered to read to the end of that sentence, you would have seen that the school dress code, which you signed at the beginning of the year, forbids not just the articles of clothing you mentioned, but any clothing likely to disrupt the educational process."

"So my T-shirt is disruptive?"

"You're damn right it is. It's a middle finger to the authority of this school and the school board, and to the values of this town."

This makes me smile. "Well, golly, sir, I had only intended it to be a show of support for my friend. But if it's all of those things as well, that's just super."

Stroudt gets very quiet. "Get out of my office and out of this school. You may return when you are appropriately dressed. And you can bet Purdue is going to hear about this."

Now, I've only been on the Purdue campus two times, but I certainly got the impression from walking around there that a TEAM TESSA shirt wouldn't cause much of a stir.

"You have a lovely afternoon, sir," I say as I exit the office.

Intrepid reporter Cindy Alpert is standing in the hallway as I exit Mr. Stroudt's office. "So what happened?" she asks.

"I got suspended because my T-shirt is disruptive to the educational process," I say. "How did you even know I was in there?"

"I didn't. I was walking by and heard yelling, and I figured there might be a story. So do you have any comment?"

"I think this school has pretty weird ideas about what's disruptive," I say, and walk out.

I'm just clearing the parking lot when I hear footsteps running behind me. I turn around, prepared to fight, and I see Tessa.

"Did you just get suspended?" she asks, her eyes wide.

I look at my TEAM TESSA shirt. "Yep."

She throws my nasty jersey with the red goo on it at me. And now I have red goo on my TEAM TESSA shirt.

"Damn it, Luke! Do not go getting in trouble for me! It's not gonna prove anything to me if you lose your scholarship! It's bad enough *my* life is ruined!" She's crying. I have an instinct to hug her, but it doesn't feel quite right. So I put a hand on her shoulder.

"T, I kind of hate to admit this, but I'm not doing this for you. I mean, I am. But I'm also doing it for me. It turns out that I sleep a lot better when I know I'm doing the right thing. Not that I've had a lot of opportunity to test that recently. But I'm hoping."

"Well, go take a nap, then. You look like hell."

"Thanks! 'Preciate it!" I say, smiling. I start walking away, and Tessa calls after me.

"Lucas!"

"Yeah?"

"Thank you."

"I ... You really shouldn't thank me. I'm ... I was supposed to be your friend. I'm really late to this party."

"Well," Tessa says, "I'm glad you finally showed up." She turns and walks away.

— — — — — —

There's not much to do at home, so I decide to stop by the library. Cindy Alpert already has the story posted on the *Bee*: Star Athlete Suspended for T-Shirt. It features a photo of me in my shirt. I'm not sure I qualify as a star athlete. It's not like I play basketball or football.

"This school has funny ideas about what's disruptive," student in TEAM TESSA shirt says.

I smile.

I check Facebook and find I've been tagged in a photo. It's the photo of me from the *Bee*.

And I've already got ten messages asking where people can get their own TEAM TESSA shirts. And an invitation to like a page called "Save Giant Brooks!"

I click on the page and see that two thousand people like it. Well, that's cool. I hope they all decide to buy their groceries there.

I check back on the *Bee* because, for the first time in a really long time, I'm kind of proud of myself, and I just want to read the article again. I get this: "Error 404: the page you are looking for is not at this address." So they've taken down the *Bee*. I hope Cindy didn't get suspended too.

I walk home, wash off my TEAM TESSA shirt in the sink, and hang it up to dry next to the window. When it's time to go to work two hours later, my shirt is dry. I pull it on and head out my front door. Which, since I got home, has acquired the word FAG in pink spray paint. Fortunately, I still have the jersey that Tessa threw at me, adorned with the number I got when I made varsity in ninth grade: 12. I fold the jersey in half and tack it on the front door, so now our front door says FIG.

When I get to work, I get this text from Tessa: "Your front door says fig. Very dadaist."

I have no idea what the hell she's talking about. But at least she's talking to me. Or, anyway, texting me. Assuming nobody torches our apartment, I might actually get a good night's sleep tonight.

21

Tessa

Most friends don't remember the actual first time they met because usually it's a gradual thing, like you happened to sit next to each other in class one day and then the next day, too, or you worked at Scoops Ice Cream one summer and by the end of your shifts you were close to the other employees, but you don't know the moment.

My friendship with Lucas is different that way.

We have a photograph from our first conversation.

If I were in English class I would turn it in as a decent representation of irony since it's a black-and-white picture from the *Brookfield Tribune*, back before we had to combine school districts because of lack of funding and people moving away because the auto industry tanked.

My desk is a slab of Formica on two filing cabinets.

The Lucas picture is framed, positioned between a family photo of Danny, Dad, Mom, and me in Jackson Hole, Wyoming, dressed as cowboys, which is only mildly embarrassing now, and a photo I took of Josie when my parents found an old Polaroid camera and it turned out to have film inside. She's only half there in the picture because I wasn't really trying to have her pose; I was just checking to see if the camera worked. Sure enough, the warped photo spat out and a few seconds later there Josie was, heading out the staff door into the bright, cold January air.

I'm getting ready for work with my nerves sprinting because my parents are downstairs arguing about money and I can hear words like "closing," "mortgage," "financial aid," and "bankruptcy" and I try to drown them out with Josie's mix. I turn up the volume on the French song and pick up Josie's picture, thumbing the warped edge. She's looking over her shoulder at me, caught somewhere between a grin and a seductive glance, and her hair is outlined in white from the snowy background. Her purple cat-eye glasses perch on her head as though she has an extra set of eyes up there. The whole thing has an otherwordly look to it, like something found in an attic from another era. Partially this is because the film was, like, decades old, but it's also due to the fact that Josie and I are sort of stop-start-stop. Like sprints on the track. You get ready and give it everything and then it's over. Or maybe that's wrong because we haven't given it—us—a real shot because there's too much mayhem around. Either way, when the mix slides into the song, pumping out the lyrics "I wanna I wanna I wanna be adored," it occurs to me that maybe Josie and I are in two different places: she's ready to be adored and I'm just ready not to be loathed. Adoration sounds good, but impossible with the click of cameras and flashbulbs, and reporters everywhere.

And yet, that's exactly how Lucas and I found each other. I hold the frame in my hands, staring at the image, letting myself get sucked into the pixels. We are so young, he is all limbs, his hair sticking up at the back. My hair is blunt, to my chin, and I'm taller than he is, with bigger shoes, which was a competitive thing back then. Anyone looking at the picture would think that we are reaching for each other, our arms stretched out, fingers spread. But a closer look reveals that in midair between us is a can of frozen lemonade. It is the same can that Lucas took from the display my parents had set up for the grand opening of their new store—the one that had been such big news for our area that reporters as far away as Indianapolis had come to wolf down cut sandwiches and cold sodas. But Lucas's mom had forbidden soda, so in an act of young rebellion, he'd poached a display can of semifrozen pink lemonade and—his arm was great even then—thrown it hard . . . right into my back. Pain and surprise zinged through me and I spun around, searching for the source, and found Lucas, horrified that he'd hurt me, and the can sweating into the grass at my feet. Lucas was so sorry and

I was so surprised that we started to laugh, which turned into red-faced hysterics as we began a game of catch. I remember that my fingers stung from the cold, and that Lucas kept count of how many successful passes we had, and how we talked as the rest of the celebration went on without us as we got absorbed in our own game. The photograph was taken without us knowing. My parents snipped it from the paper and framed one copy for them and one copy for Mrs. Fogelman. The picture migrated over the years, from the kitchen counter to the hallway. Now my room.

"Tessa!" my father shouts over the music. I can't actually hear my name, just the sound of his voice. "Tessa!"

I put the picture back. It's time to go.

— — — — — —

I've never been out of the country, but I've seen pictures of crowded India and of the Beatles landing in London, and while my arrival at Giant Brooks isn't met with adoring fans, it is as big a crowd as I remember seeing. At least around here.

"Is it true that Giant Brooks is minutes away from going under?"

A reporter shoves her face in front of my mother's as she gets out of the car. My father shoots her a look that says, "Don't say a word." Since my parents are silent, the crowd turns on me.

There are supporters carrying signs that read SAVE

GIANT BROOKS. There are others holding aloft poster-board with TEAM TESSA written in thick marker—some rainbow-colored—and a bunch of people who are sure not from Brookfield-Mason. They have expensive shoes and good hair and wave to me as I walk toward the entrance.

But there are double that number of signs that say GO AWAY, TACKLE TEAM TESSA (that's the entire football team in full force and uniform), SIN SPREADS, GIANT BROOKS = GIANT GAY.

"Can a store even *be* gay?" I ask Josie when I see her inside. She's doing inventory of the bags of charcoal, which involves lifting and isn't much fun, so she hardly gives a laugh.

"This town blows," she says under her breath as she heaves another bag on top of a pile.

I do a quick check of the angry crowd outside, the deserted aisles at the store my parents built from nothing—the one that has paid for my running shoes, my allowance, and lots of the salaries in this town—and start to nod. But something keeps me from totally giving in. "It's not all bad," I say.

"You're too forgiving," Josie says. Her voice is hard. Flat. She sighs and pushes her glasses up with her pointer finger.

"Come on, Josie." I try to make a face to lighten the mood even though I feel like I'm trapped under water.

She gives her head a defeated shake. "Seriously, Tessa, the rest of the world isn't like this."

Now I feel something aside from down and worried.

I feel annoyed. "But it is like this. You've lived all over, right? This is a small town. This is so much of America, Jos. You think it'd be different for me if I lived in Berlin, Arkansas? Or Lucca, Mississippi? My life would be the same there."

Josie's mouth turns down. She bites her top lip. "Well, it wouldn't have me in it if you lived there."

I see my mother waving me to the back of the store but I can't leave just yet. I bounce back and forth from one foot to the other, a habit left over from prerace warm-ups. "And that would be a good thing?" I ask.

She waits a second before responding. "Not good. That's not what I mean. More like . . . easier. For you." She loads another bag of charcoal, scraping it on the linoleum until I help her lift it. Across the weight of it, Josie looks at me, her eyes not sad exactly, but sorry for what she's about to say. "You would have dealt with this eventually. I know that. But I can't help but feel like it's because of me that it turned into a complete circus. Look at them out there. Crazy people. I mean, I don't even feel safe driving alone. Or walking to the post office."

I crack a smile, fighting off tears. "What are you mailing?"

Josie gets flustered for a second, half laughing. Then she drops her end of the bag and it lands with a thud. "It's not that I don't like you. I did. I do. It's just . . ." Her gaze goes to the parking lot, where people have walked right up to the plate-glass window and shoved their signs at us.

I know she told Luke how great she thinks I am. Now I realize this might have been her parting words.

"It feels like too much, you know?" Josie fidgets with her hair.

And I want to say I don't know, that she's the one who helped me go forward, that I like her songs and her smile and the way she kisses. But I don't. "I know what you mean," I say, and before I actually cry, I walk over and hug her. Right with everyone watching, which of course only makes the shouting and cheering louder. Josie's right. We're a spectacle, not a couple.

"This doesn't mean I won't help you," she says. "You know, if they reinstate Prom or whatever."

I nod and walk the long way through the frozen foods to the back of the store.

———— —— —— —— —— ——

"Aren't we a big bunch of sad sacks?" My mother has her apron on inside out as she methodically places napkins—the good, double-ply, expensive ones—into a cardboard box that once held Lucky Charms.

I nod and start to help her. "No," she says, and directs me to another empty box. "Make yourself useful and bring the salsa and chips here."

"How many?" I ask.

"All of it," she says. "The whole aisle."

I stare, amazed. "Huh?"

My mother is all business. "When times are tight, you

make adjustments. The yacht club called and—well, they were probably feigning support—but they asked if we'd sell them paper goods at cut-rate."

"Mom—"

"Don't Mom me. We're still making money off it, which may not be the case forever."

"And the salsa?"

She shrugs. "Breaking even. But it's got a long shelf life and they'll probably use it all up this summer, so it's not going to waste or anything . . ."

I spend the next hour or so of my shift lugging boxes of salsa to the delivery van. Once the whole lot of Pedro's and El Guapo and the unlikely Midwestern Salsa Company are out, I start with the chips. I only pop one bag, which is the hazard of carrying too many at a time.

"Need a hand?" Danny steps on the chips I dropped which means cleanup in aisle six but also means he can drive with me to the yacht club.

"Yes. I need many hands," I say, and together we pile stuff into the van and ignore the protesters who have found us in the back loading area.

Danny looks at me across the van's bucket seats but doesn't hassle me until we're parked at the yacht club's delivery door. "I hate this place," Danny says. "It's so wannabe fancy. Like the trellis. What is a trellis, anyway? Who needs it?"

"People who like flowers. Or who have weddings here," I say, as I bring in a box of salsa and put it in the dark corridor near the industrial kitchen. "I always kind of liked this place." I look at the groomed shrubs, the newly varnished decking, the maintenance crew painting the railings white like they do every spring.

In the middle of unloading, Danny strips his polo shirt off and reveals a bright purple T-shirt. "TEAM TESSA?" I ask.

He grins. "I'm MVP," he says.

"'Course you are," I say, and close the van door, catching my thumb in the handle in the process. Danny laughs and it feels good just to have a normal brother-sister moment. You know, with a brother laughing at a sister's pain.

"Ahem." The throat clearing comes from Mrs. Elaine Gertrin, who wears her yacht club blazer and pressed red trousers as though she's about to aye-aye us.

"We brought the stuff from Giant Brooks," Danny says as Mrs. Gertrin stands there.

"Yes," she says, her lips pinched and her raven eyes not moving from my face.

"And the napkins," I say. My feet start bouncing and in a minute I know I'll start sweating and wishing I were in a crowd of loud, angry protesters instead of under this woman's intense gaze. "You always want napkins."

Danny takes my lead. "Yeah, napkins are key. Can't really eat without 'em. Well, you can, I mean, I do all the time but—"

"You're very . . . prompt," Mrs. Gertrin says, like that explains why we're standing here. "I'll forward payment once we check the stock."

Danny wipes his upper lip with the back of his hand.

"We're supposed to get it now." He looks at me and then at her. "Sort of standard, you know?"

More throat clearing. "Yes. Well."

Danny puts out a hand. His TEAM TESSA shirt is bright in the sun, dampening around the *T* and the *M*.

Mrs. Gertrin disappears without explanation and we wait, leaning on the van until it gets too hot. "Two more seconds and I'm going in," Danny says.

"What's her problem?" I ask, like we both aren't perfectly aware of it.

Mrs. Gertrin comes out with an envelope. "You'll find the exact amount is in here," she says. "Check."

"Never mind," Danny says, and shoves the envelope in his back pocket without checking, just to make a point. Then we leave, driving back to the store in air-conditioned silence.

The quiet is broken of course by the ranting and raving at the store. "What gives?" Danny asks, cupping his hands to see why the crowd has grown even larger.

I reach for the envelope and then, just because I know Mom and Dad need to make a deposit, I open it up. "Danny . . . ," I start.

"Check it out!" Danny says, reaching for the door handle.

"No, Danny—wait!" I grab his shoulder and stop him. I show him the check.

It takes only a few seconds for Danny to reach the same conclusion I did. The check is for a few thousand dollars. It is from the personal account of Mrs. Himmelrath.

"You don't think—" Danny looks like his dog was just hit by our van.

I nod. "She's doing it. I know it. Jenny Himmelrath's mother is throwing a Prom. A *private* Prom." As soon as the words are out, I feel sick. I start to put my head down so I don't pass out when Danny tugs at my hand.

"Tessa."

"Leave me alone," I say. "I can't do this anymore." Josie can't. I can't. My family can't.

"Tessa," Danny says, insisting. "Check it out."

So I look up because I have nothing else to do, nothing left to say. At the front of Giant Brooks, right where our lake chairs and grills usually go, is a booth. Only this one isn't selling summer charcoal or bug spray. My father and mother, my mom standing on an upturned milk crate, are waving things in the air, shouting. I can't help but start to smile through my tears.

My parents are selling purple TEAM TESSA T-shirts.

And people are buying them.

22

>◀

LUKE

I got a one-day suspension for wearing a TEAM TESSA shirt. The next day, they sent five kids home for wearing them. And the day after that, when thirty kids showed up in them, the administration just gave in.

So on day four, I wear mine again, and it feels pretty good. Actually it feels great. Those of us in the shirts are still way less than half or even a third of the people at school, but it is really nice to be able to look around in the hall or any class you happen to be in and know that the entire world isn't against you. Maybe three-quarters of the world—or at least of the school—but the important part is not feeling alone. Whenever I see another person wearing a TEAM TESSA shirt, we lock eyes for a second and exchange a smile. Usually right before someone "accidentally" knocks into us.

Tessa made me watch *West Side Story* once. We both

talked about how beautiful Natalie Wood was in that movie pretty much the whole time, and yeah, I suppose that should have been a clue, but what can I say, it's really hard to see something when you're not looking for it. Or, I guess, when you're looking for its opposite.

Anyway, it's a corny old movie that I didn't really like all that much except for the beautiful–Natalie Wood part, but I'm thinking about it a lot today as Team Tessa walks around in its gang colors, exchanging hostile looks with the enemy gang that's on our turf. Or maybe we're on their turf. Or maybe it's both of our turfs.

It's not quite Sharks versus Jets around here yet, though. For one thing, the other gang can't quite agree on their uniform. I've seen a few TEAM JESUS shirts, one NORMAL AND PROUD one, and one that says THIS IS INDIANA, NOT SAN FRANCISCO, which is a not-very-catchy slogan that's both hard to say and hard to figure out.

The other reason things haven't reached *West Side Story* levels of deadliness, apart from the fact that nobody is spontaneously breaking into song, is that the tension level has gone way down. Sure, there are still people bodychecking me into lockers, and so many people have written "fag" on my locker that I've stopped trying to clean it off (though I do still patrol Tessa's locker pretty vigilantly, and nothing stays on there for more than two class periods), but that feeling from the first couple of days—like any random person might explode in a spree of hate crimes at any moment—has gone away.

Of course, it took all of about twenty-five minutes to find out about the Himmelraths' "Go Straight to Prom" event at the yacht club. It's not an official school event, true, but almost everyone will be there. There will be girls shaking it to the secular sounds of Miss Kaboom in revealing dresses, bad food, and plenty of spots at the yacht club for people to sneak away and pour some of their mom's vodka into a glass of punch, or smoke a quick joint, or just cop a feel. Yep, it should be a wholesome family event.

And yet, I wish I could go. I wouldn't betray Tessa again even if I were invited, which I'm sure I'm not, but still. I mean, I do live in this town. As much as I try to resist it, I'm not immune to the idea that Prom is an important ritual of being a teenager. Hell, that's why I asked the girl I loved to go with me by using a big lighted sign. And now it's something I don't get to do. I don't get to do it with school because people are stupid and narrow-minded, and I don't get to do it with my classmates because I stood up, however weakly and late, for my friend. Well, I guess I deserve it. It feels, in a way, like a just punishment—not for standing up for Tessa but for failing to stand up for her. Oh hell, I guess I can admit it, it's punishment for standing against her when she needed me.

Someone left their invitation lying out in the weight room. I pick it up and look it over: "Go *Straight* to Prom! Come as God made and intended you." I don't know what to think about God—Mom always says the people who talk loudest about their faith are the ones least likely to be living it—and since we never go to church or anything, it just never seemed like an urgent question to me. Yeah, I have been involved in team prayers before games, and I certainly enjoy a moment of quiet before I have to pitch, but I never really thought a high school baseball game was something God, if he exists, would really have the time to care about.

So like I said, I haven't thought about this question a lot, but I really want to ask somebody: Don't you think God made Tessa this way? Because who the hell would choose this if they didn't have to? I know Tessa is stubborn, but she'd never throw her whole family, their business, and her college fund into jeopardy unless it was something she had to do.

The whole thing kind of makes me sad. One thing that's cool about the official school Prom is that, unlike every other party, the cool kids can't exclude anyone. Even the most unpopular kid in school can get dressed up and go pretend to have fun right alongside the popular kids. Well, not this year, I guess.

After my workout I shower and head over to Giant Brooks.

The parking lot is packed with pro- and anti-Tessa factions. There are Ohio, Illinois, and Kentucky license plates in the parking lot. It looks like there's a pretty steady flow of people shopping, which is good. I haven't been able to get back to the library to continue my Facebook plan on behalf of Giant Brooks, but it looks like other people have taken up the baton.

Right by the front door, there is a table staffed by none other than Kate Sweeney. She's managing a huge crowd of people lined up to buy T-shirts. Most are TEAM TESSA shirts, but there are also some that read SHOP GIANT BROOKS: GOOD FOOD FOR EVERYONE.

I shoot Kate a puzzled look and she smiles at me. I head inside to the office to punch in. Since I'm no longer ashamed to face Tessa's folks, I peek my head into the office and see Tessa behind her dad's desk. "Um. Hey," I say. "You in charge today, or what?"

She looks up and smiles. "Yeah. Mom and Dad are at a UPS Store doing fulfillment on the e-commerce part of the business."

"I don't know what the hell you're talking about."

"They're shipping T-shirts. All over the place. Once people saw them on the news, everybody wanted one. Well, not everybody. But a lot of people. Enough that it looks like we're not going to lose the store."

"Well," I say, "that's good." I'm too ashamed to say anything else.

I try to think of what it would mean to Brookfield if Giant Brooks closed. I kind of feel like it would be the last nail in the coffin of this town with the dead Main Street. And I almost caused that. Suddenly I don't feel like I can look Tessa in the eye. The floor is pretty interesting in here, so I start examining it.

"Lucas—" she says, and then stops.

"Well, I guess I'm gonna go stock some shelves—" I start. I still can't look at her.

"Lucas, I just want you to know . . ." I look up at her, and she's looking at me with tears in her eyes. I look at the floor again and wonder if there's any way for me to just sink right through it.

"Um. I was. I mean, you . . ." I trail off.

"I want you to know," Tessa starts again, her voice stronger this time. And then she pauses again. "That Kate could use some help at the T-shirt table. So why don't you go help her after you punch in."

"Um. Okay." I kind of want to talk to my best friend, Tessa, about this girl I think I probably have a crush on, but it's like I don't really have a best friend anymore. I slink out of the office and head up to the table.

"Oh my God, I'm so glad you're here," Kate says when she sees me. "It's been crazy—completely nonstop since I got here."

"I didn't think you worked here anymore," I say.

"I didn't. But, you know, with my T-shirt-selling expertise from working at Wild Thingz!, I'm kind of a natural for the job. Plus I set up the website for them."

"You're a woman of many talents," I say.

"You have no idea," she says, smiling, and I'm really glad there are a ton of people here buying T-shirts, because I have no response to that.

My shift flies by because so many people want to

buy shirts, and pretty soon it's closing time at Giant Brooks.

"Um," I say to Kate, "do you want to, um . . . get some ice cream or something?"

She smiles. "Yeah. I'd like that." I'm relieved that she doesn't ask whether it's a date or mock me for taking so long to ask her out or anything.

We head back to the office to punch out. The door is closed, but I can hear Tessa's raised voice behind it. "Really? Are you really saying that to me right now?"

Kate and I walk away, and I say, "You know, I kind of wish I could just knock on the door and make sure everything's okay."

Kate looks at me. "That girl eats broken glass and spits nails. I'm pretty sure she doesn't need you to protect her."

I laugh at the description. Is that how people see Tessa? "I know she doesn't need my protection. But she might need my support. You know? It's just weird. She was the most important person in my life for as long as I can remember, and now I can't even really talk to her. Not like we used to, anyway."

"Yeah. I'm familiar with that. Have you noticed me hanging with all my high school friends this summer?"

"Nope."

"That's because we're growing apart. We're not the same people we were at fourteen. So maybe that's how life is, you know? You change, other people change, and people come in and out of your life."

I think about that for a minute. Maybe she's right. She's older and wiser than me. But I'm just not ready to give up my friendship with Tessa yet. But I decide I'm a little tired of thinking about the whole thing. "So, what's Purdue like?" I ask.

Kate's face lights up. "Hey! You've discovered a new topic of conversation! Good for you!" Not that many people can get away with teasing me without pissing me off. But Kate is definitely on the list.

We walk over to the Dairy Barn. We're in line for soft serve when Steve Sedacca walks by us with two giant-size chocolate-dip cones. "Sweeney!" he says, smiling. Then he looks at me. "You some kind of fag hag now?"

"As a matter of fact, she is," I say. "I give her fashion tips, we talk about how guys are jerks, stuff like that."

Steve certainly wasn't expecting that, so all he can respond with is, "Well, see ya, Sweeney."

"Always a pleasure," Kate says, and we laugh. We get some ice cream, and, not wanting to sit here and wait for all the Steve Sedaccas in town to come up and say nasty things to us, we start walking back toward Giant Brooks. She tells me which dorms are the best, which core classes are the worst, and which fraternities I should avoid pledging (in her opinion, all of them).

As we're walking back to the parking lot so Kate can get her car, we're both swinging our arms, and our hands kind of touch, and then our fingers are threaded together. It's weird. When guys are bragging in the locker room, nobody ever talks about getting some hand-holding action. But it feels really good. And, I mean, it's one thing to kiss somebody behind a tree at a kegger and another thing to intertwine your fingers out on the street where anyone could see you and run to everybody else talking about what it means.

I don't know what it means. If anything.

"You want a ride?" Kate says.

"Sure," I say. "I live on Main Street."

We don't say anything for most of the ride back to my house. "God, Main Street just makes me so sad these days," Kate says. "Remember when we were little, and people used to walk up and down and say hi to each other and stuff? Maybe it's just nostalgia for being a little kid, but I feel like Main Street used to be the best part of living here. Now it's just a bunch of empty stores. Somebody ought to do something with it."

"Somebody should," I say.

The car stops, and I'm not sure if I'm supposed to try to kiss her or not. "So this is it," I say, pointing at my door.

"Okay," Kate says.

I don't get out of the car. I look at her. She's looking at me. And before I can think about it too much, I give her a quick kiss. On the lips.

"Thanks for the ride," I say, hopping out of the car.

"Thanks for the kiss," she says.

"Anytime!" I say. I bound up the steps to my apartment, and I guess maybe I'm a little loud.

"Is that a herd of elephants, or is it my son?" Mom's groggy voice calls. "Because if it's not the elephants, somebody's in trouble."

"Sorry, Mom!" I call out.

"Stop sounding so chipper. I'm trying to sleep," she says.

Just then, my phone gives a loud beep.

"Really?" Mom says.

"I'm really sorry," I say, fumbling with the phone to put it on vibrate.

I look at the phone. It's not from Kate, whose number, for some stupid reason, I still don't have. I don't know why I got my hopes up. It's from Tessa.

"Can I talk to you?" it says.

23

Tessa

Lucas is out of breath when he calls, like he's just run up two flights of stairs or been chased. "Hey," he says.

"Are you smiling?" I ask.

"You can seriously tell that over the phone?" I hear him runnng water. We used to be the kind of friends who could pee on the phone and not be grossed out. Now Lucas stops the water running.

"So . . . ," I start.

"So . . . ," he says back, and waits for me to say something.

And I want to tell him—what? What do I want to say? Thanks? Or, I miss you? I used to be able to say anything to this guy and now it all feels so loaded and heavy and like there's this ravine between us and I can't figure out how to make it over to where he is.

"How's Josie?" he asks, finally, trying to fill the void.

"Uh, fine, I think."

"Oh. You're not—"

I shake my head as though he can see me. "No."

This conversation isn't happening the way I wanted it to. "I just . . . I texted because . . ."

Lucas clears his throat. "Come on, Tess."

"Look," I say, annoyed now. "You're the grand-gesture person. Not me."

"Step up to the plate, Masterson," Lucas says.

And just like that I'm pissed again. "Never mind."

"Don't tell me to never mind. I'm like . . . the king of minding."

"Yup, that's you. The mayor of the grand gesture."

Lucas sucks in air and I bet his mouth is all pinched and his eyebrows crumpled together. "You know what? Grand gestures are a good thing, Tessa. They're dramatic. They're . . ." He pauses, maybe remembering his failed grand gesture with me. "They might not always get you what you want. But they're real. Maybe you'll try it some time."

We hang up and I'm bubbling over with frustration. I'm not the big-gesture type. And he knows that. I don't even like karaoke for God's sake. But when I look in the mirror I feel really bad because I'm still in my TEAM TESSA T-shirt. The one Lucas is responsible for. I pull it off, crumple it up, and whip it into the hamper. There's no one there to cheer as I make the shot.

— — — — — —

In the morning, I have that thirty-second grace period, pre-waking, when I still think everything's normal. Back the way it was. I stretch my toes out so they curl over the end of the bed, and lift my head as the clock comes into view. Ten minutes to get up, shower, and get to work.

"Tessa!" Danny shouts.

It's like any other morning, when Danny's busy shoving bagels into his mouth and waiting for me. I decide not to shower since everyone already thinks I'm a social outcast. Then I ignore the TEAM TESSA shirt and just focus on shorts and a shirt and pulling my hair back as I trot down the stairs in search of a frozen waffle to eat unthawed in the car. Lucas used to keep a stash of Eggos in his freezer even though he is against frozen breakfast food as a rule. I feel a twinge as I picture him throwing the waffle to me Frisbee style all spring and how I kept gummy worms in my bag just for him even though candy for breakfast isn't my idea of great nutrition.

"Tessa!" Danny bellows again, and before I can thwack him for being brotherly and annoying, I realize he's trying to warn me.

In the kitchen, next to the open window with its flimsy yellow curtains, and right near our toaster, my parents stand with their arms around each other like a bizzarro version of that painting we studied in AP History, *American Gothic*. Mom's in a too-big TEAM TESSA shirt and Dad's in one that's slightly too small and you can see his gut, but they are united as parents.

But they're not looking at me.

Or at Danny.

They're focused on the two television cameras aimed at them.

The same ones that turn to capture footage of me.

"Can you come down the stairs again?" one of the crew asks.

"What?" I ask, trying to make sense of it all.

"Mr. Wekstein did a live interview," my father says. "On *The Morning Show* in New York!"

"New York!" My mom beams like it's a foreign language. A foreign planet. Maybe it is.

A reporter comes in the front door, the one we never use, and wipes her high heels on our oval braided rug even though she doesn't have anything on the bottom of her shoes, and if she did we wouldn't care.

"Hi, Tessa!" She sticks her hand out and I automatically shake it. "I'm Louise Madden."

And of course I know who she is. She's on TV. Every morning. Only now she's in my house and smiling at me with her perfectly outlined lips and expensively cut pantsuit and coiffed hair while I stand unshowered and craving a frozen waffle.

"Let's back up, Lou. Introduce again and we'll get her coming down the stairs."

I allow myself to be directed: down the stairs, meeting Louise, hugging my parents, high-fiving with Danny, who gives me his I'm-about-to-crack-up face. I chew my lip to avoid laughing or screaming.

"Ah, I have to go work," I say.

"Perfect," Louise Madden says to the camera guy. "We can cut from there to the supermarket."

"I have footage of MegaMart and a statement from Corporate," she adds, like we're not all standing here.

And I know I should be jumping for joy that "my cause" has gone viral. That I'm somehow the voice of people who need one.

"So, Tessa," Louise says, "let's get your response to the results of the ACLU action."

I feel dumb because I've been so busy moping about Josie and wallowing about Lucas that I haven't been paying attention to much of anything. "Ah . . ."

Sensing that I'm clueless, Louise says, "The statement just came this morning—as your mother was saying. Mr. Wekstein announced live that Brookfield-Mason agreed to create a policy protecting students from discrimination on the basis of sexual orientation and gender identity."

"Wow!" I say. I smile and my parents give me a thumbs-up. But there should be more.

And I know what's missing.

But I can't do it. I'm not that girl.

In the glowy morning light in the kitchen that always made me feel protected and warm, Louise shakes her head at the cameras like I've totally failed. "We'll get a statement later."

— — — — — —

I'm on deli duty, my first time since Josie ended things, and the smell of salty ham slices makes me wish I hadn't raided the frozen-food aisles for whole-wheat waffles.

"Excuse me."

I know the voice even before I see the face it comes from so I move extra slowly, taking the ham from the slicer and following store protocol by triple-wrapping it in plastic film and putting it back in the cold case with its meaty friends.

"How can I help you, Jenny?" I ask, going back to my original customer-satisfaction training and "personalizing my interaction" by using her first name.

Jenny Himmelrath tilts her head, the silver of her headband glints in the fluorescent lights.

"I wonder if you could be so kind as to fill an order for me," she says, firing her own retail training right back at me.

"Why, I'd be honored," I say.

It's a war of the fake, overly nice people.

"We need fifteen platters of deli rolls," she says.

I stand on tiptoe so I can look more closely at her over the barrier of the counter. "Seriously, Jenny? Fifteen?"

"What?" She shrugs. "I thought you'd be glad for the business."

Jenny looks around, perfectly composed, her hair smooth and her hands on her hips. I follow her gaze to the rest of the store. It's not full by any means but it's not nearly as desolate as it has been. We're getting new products in, and a few major brands have ponied up to add bright displays, wanting to "be associated with a store that supports the American value of nondiscrimination." This is particularly amusing because there are just as many brands who have pulled their distribution and cases because they "only want to be featured in stores that support American values." They're now at MegaMart.

"We don't *need* the business," I say. Then I take a breath. "Okay, just tell me what you'd like and if there are any food allergies."

"For meat?" Jenny makes a face.

"The Paulson's poultry comes in contact with their peanut-processing plant so I like to be clear about that," I say.

Jenny stares at me. And stares. And stares until I raise my eyebrows at her.

"That's, like, so . . . nice of you," she says.

Now it's my turn to shrug. "It's just store policy. Full disclosure. Taking care of our patrons," I tell her.

She hands me an order slip written in her curvy script. It's on yacht club stationery.

"Did you know I'm, like, deathly allergic to tree nuts and legumes?" Jenny asks, her voice hushed.

"I didn't." The slip tells me I'll be slicing smoked turkey and Genoa salami all day. "Do you want these arranged in a party-platter format?" I get the booklet and show her the fancy toothpicks, the unfurled lettuce as a base.

"I, like, nearly died two years ago," she says. In her

eyes I see something I've never seen before. "No one really gets it. One minute you're fine and just a regular cheerleader and the next you eat one stupid cookie and blow up like a frickin' helium balloon." She moves her hands over her face. "I couldn't breathe. At all."

"That sounds really scary," I say, because obviously it does and the fact that this girl has hated me forever doesn't mean that much right now. In fact, as I watch her watch me, we're both doing that thing where we acknowledge that we're both just regular people. Regular people with issues.

"I'll keep the platters completely nut-free." I point behind me. "See? That slicer doesn't ever get any Paulson's on it. So no cross-contaminants."

Jenny's eyes light up as though I've told her she's lost weight or whatever is usually top of her list of wants. "No cross-contaminants. Cool."

She could wander the store while I spend the time slicing the turkey and other meats, but she doesn't. She watches me.

And then it hits me. Maybe this is all it would take. Jenny Himmelrath and her peanut-allergic self could be my grand statement.

So when I finish the first platter and it's cloaked in plastic wrap and looking very fancy, I hold it out to her. "This'll go in the big fridge," I say. "But I wanted you to see it first. Just so you can tell what the final product will be."

Jenny smiles. A real smile. And I know it'll work. If I can just ask her.

I put the tray away. "Before I get to the other ones," I say, rallying up my nerve to ask, "I was just wondering . . ."

"Yeah." She leans on the counter, aware of the television cameras off in the distance.

"Actually, do you mind if I . . ." I wave Louise over and there's a bunch of noise and confusion as I start the next platter and Jenny signs a release form for being filmed and they set up.

Talk about grand gestures, I think. This is it.

The cameras set up the shot, angling so they get my apron and the unattractive yet nut-free wedge of brined turkey as well as Jenny's "camera-ready" short shorts and pert smile.

"So, Jenny," I say.

"Tessa," she says back.

"Now that we're . . ." I stumble over the words. What are we? Nothing still. Not friends. But . . . something? "Tell me where these platters are headed."

Jenny stands up straight, gleaming. "My mother has organized a wonderful event. At the yacht club. And we're supporting our local store by buying extra platters." She pauses, looking at me for a sign she's said the correct thing.

And she has. But not the thing I wanted.

So I try again. "And this event—is it open to the public?"

Strike. Jenny looks annoyed. "Well, the yacht club is an exclusive venue—"

With all my might I try not to react. I try to do what I do when I'm running and just forget my environment and focus on some invisible dot in the distance.

But Jenny clicks into what's happening and looks genuinely horrified. "Oh, gosh. You didn't think . . ." She puts her hand to her mouth. "I'm just here for the platters, okay?"

I take a gasping breath and don't make a bigger fool of myself by asking directly if I can go to the dance. If maybe Lucas and I could go as a couple there. Not a couple couple but as . . . us. Jenny doesn't magically hand me an engraved invite.

She just looks awkward and says, "I renege on the filming stuff."

Louise tries to talk her out of it but Jenny fires up with how she's still a minor for another three weeks and then, once I have the platters all set, Jenny comes up to me.

"They look really nice."

I nod.

She wants to add something but doesn't seem to know what. So she asks, "What's the most expensive item here? Like in the whole store."

I shrug. "I . . . don't know. I guess I never thought about it."

"Well, whatever it is, we'll take two—no, five—of them!" She claps her hands conspiratorially.

— — — — — —

I'm out back sharing chips and a giant bottle of grape soda with Danny when the television cameras find us and start filming.

"So, Tessa, let's try the shot again," the perfectly coiffed reporter says. "Think about what you'd like the television audience to know." And to the camera guys she adds, "We'll splice it in. And try to get a shot of the back here. It's so small-town."

I look to where she's pointing. The delivery docks. The old asphalt where Josie and I played four square last fall, when I knew I had a crush on her. The spot where my mother fell and broke her tailbone on the ice. The steps where Lucas and I sat hugging when we both got into college. Where he cried about his dad. The sign on which he made his grand gesture.

"So, Tessa . . ." Louise waits.

Danny looks at me.

Each stalk of corn in the distance seems like it's waiting for me to deliver the ultimate sentence.

"I . . ."

I look at Danny but he can't do this for me.

I think about how I still wanted to go to that stupid yacht club dance even though it's organized against me. Even though I'm exactly who they don't want there.

And I feel so dumb for wanting to dance in a tux. With a girl.

And then I feel even worse because I still want to do both of those things.

And I don't have Lucas next to me to hold my hand until I get the courage to do it.

"She's not up to this," Louise says.

And Louise is right.

I watch them pack up their equipment. Watch the cameras being loaded into the van, Louise talking on her multiple phones and texting on her Blackberry at the same time, watch my parents try not to look sad for me.

Danny punches my shoulder like the good sport he is. "Next time," he says.

I nod. Louise shakes my parents' hands and climbs into the van which revs up and pulls out right under the sign that reads SAVE GIANT BROOKS.

And I think immediately about the last song on Josie's mix, the one that goes "You gotta change yourself before you go trying to change the world."

I stand up, springing into action before the van signals left to turn onto the highway. And I run. I run fast because I can, because I need to. Sprinting to the van, I pound on the side. "Wait."

Louise has the window down before the van's halted.

"I do. I do have something."

And right there, without proper lighting or fake setup, one of the camera guys films me. And I say how everyone thinks it's about the dance. I clear my thoat, still a little out of breath. "Or about being, you know, gay. Or, um, a lesbian."

It's the first time I've said it out loud and it doesn't feel as weird as I thought it would. "But the thing is . . . it's more than that." I pause and the reporter gets nudgy, tapping her fingers on the windowsill, and the camera guy's doing that thing with his finger meaning "We're rolling here, she better say something interesting." So I say this: "My parents have a store they love and people who support them and that's been an amazing thing to see."

"We can cut to a good shot of that—the rallying. And stock footage of the packed aisles," the camera guy says.

"And the people who are against all this . . . I get it. I do. And they can have their fancy dance at the yacht club—" I try not to, but I start to tear up. "I have a friend—"

"Girlfriend?"

I shoot Louise a look. "A friend. A best friend." I start to grin through the tears. "He's the kind of guy who gives you the last bite of his ice cream cone because it's so clearly the best part. And he comes to every track meet even though—I admit it—being a runner is fun but watching runners can be tedious." I look at the camera now. "This is a friend—a boy—who knows that a grand gesture, like publicly asking a girl to Prom is a risk and might not turn out how you think. But this guy, Lucas, is the best friend I could ever have. And he thinks I'm too private for a grand gesture myself, but I'm not." I take a deep breath and chew my top lip and stare right at the camera. "Lucas Fogelman, I love you." I pause. "And just so you know, I would've looked pretty good standing next to you in a tux."

24

><

LUKE

So Tessa texts me: "Make sure you watch the *Morning Show* on ATN tomorrow." I do, and there she is, telling me she loves me. And I actually cry. I think about texting Tessa, but I guess this is one of those moments when you have to man up. Well, that's a dumb word for it, since it's this girl who's been more courageous than anybody else for weeks now. How about this: adult up.

So I adult up and call Tessa. "Hey," she says brightly. "Didja see it?"

"Yeah, I did. I love you too, you know."

"Yeah," she says. "I do know. So how was that for a grand gesture?"

"Pretty grand," I say. "Thank you. It means a lot to me to know that you forgive me."

"Whoa there," she says. "I said I loved you. I didn't say

anything about forgiving you." I don't say anything for a second, and she comes back with, "I'm kidding. I think the one kind of implies the other."

"Glad to hear it."

"All right, I gotta go. I've got freaking three interviews this morning. If I didn't think this would help the store, there's no way I would do it. I hate this."

"Tough to be a celebrity."

"You'll find out when you're a star pitcher." We say our good-byes and hang up. And it's funny. I used to want that. Like everybody, I guess, I had a mental picture—I'm the feared and hated closer who comes on for the Reds in the top of the ninth at Great American Ball Park in game seven of the World Series. I send the third, fourth, and fifth batters down in a row on swinging strikeouts that make the big sluggers look stupid, and the catcher rushes the mound and grabs me. The team comes pouring out of the dugout and buries me in a big celebratory pig-pile, and I'm a famous hero.

But now, after my little taste of what it's like to get all kinds of attention, to have every dumb thing you say played back to you to trip you up, I'm not so sure I really want that anymore. It kind of sucks. Maybe it won't be so bad if baseball doesn't work out for me. I'd still like to win a World Series game, but I'd also like to be able to say something stupid and have everybody forget about it.

Well, who the hell knows. I head out of the house to go to school and pause for a second on Main Street. Usually I don't even see the empty storefronts anymore, but after Kate said they were depressing (and then I kissed her! Did that really happen? And if so, what did it mean?), I'm taking a second look. Discount LiquorMart, Hailer's Drugstore, which was killed by MegaMart. And the place where Woolworth's was before it was a Foot Locker before it was nothing is the biggest, most depressing, emptiest space on the whole street.

As I walk to school, I'm still thinking about Kate's lips and how I was stupid to kiss her quickly when I probably could have kissed her nice and slow. But I'm also thinking about the things I don't like about Brookfield right now—the Go-Straight-to-Prom Prom and the empty Main Street. It is making me a lot more eager to get to Purdue in the fall. But I'm also having a brainstorm.

I can't tell Tessa yet in case it doesn't pan out.

I want to tell Kate, but I'm such an idiot that I don't even have her number. So I head over to Giant Brooks after school even though I'm not supposed to be working, and I join Kate at the T-shirt table.

"So you never called me," she says.

"So you never gave me your number," I answer.

"So you never asked for it," she counters. Well, she's got me there.

"So, can I have your number?" I ask.

"Duh. Of course you can. You're really making me work for this, you know that?"

I can feel myself blushing. "I'm just...I'm a little screwed up these days, and I guess...Can I be honest with you for a second?"

"I've been waiting for you to stop your incessant lies!" she says, and I can't help smiling.

"It's just that I kind of . . . I don't really like myself very much right now, and I don't really get why anyone else would either. Especially you."

Kate turns, and her auburn hair kind of swings, and her eyes twinkle as she smiles. "You are so cute," she says. "But really? I mean, do you really want to know?"

"Well, yeah."

"Okay. One, there's the big romantic gesture with the sign. Admittedly, you were barking up the wrong tree, but if you can do something like that once, it's possible you might do something like that again. Girls like that. Or I do, anyway. And also? Really, more important? All guys are assholes. I mean, at one time or another. But you're the first guy I ever met who knew he was an asshole and actually felt bad about it. It's pretty charming."

"Aren't you afraid I'll be an asshole again?"

"Oh, you will. You are a guy, after all. But then you'll say you're sorry and actually mean it, and then you almost certainly won't be an asshole in exactly that way again. You probably don't know how rare that is."

"I . . . um. I don't really know anything right now except that I really want to kiss you again."

She smiles. "You will. And a real kiss this time. Not that timid peck like last time. But right now, we've got customers, and as much as the Mastersons are tolerant and wonderful people, they still probably don't want their employees making out at work."

I give her a smile. "I'm off the clock," I say.

"That's more like it!" she says. "But I get off work in two hours. You wanna keep me company for a while?"

Dumb question. I sit there and work for free, selling Giant Brooks T-shirts, and when there's a lull, I tell her my plan.

"I'm thinking of having a Prom. On Main Street. In the old Foot Locker."

"Well," she says, "you have to get the okay from the property owners. Otherwise the cops will show up and break up the party, and that, trust me, is one hell of a buzz kill."

"So you don't think sneaking in and doing it would work? I mean, I happen to know that the owners will be otherwise occupied on that day."

She looks at me like I'm an idiot. "Do you think there is anyone in this town who might object to Tessa Masterson's Big Gay Prom?"

"Oh my God. That is the best name. You think I can use that?"

"You're missing the point, Luke. Even if the property owners aren't around, you can't trespass with something like this. There's too many people who want you to fail. But I tell you what—you take care of securing the space and I'll get a DJ I know from school and do the Evites and everything."

"Cool."

I know she's right about the whole trespassing thing, but I was hoping she was going to tell me something else.

Of course I know who owns the space that's not Wool-worth's or Foot Locker, and the entire block I live on: Mom writes a rent check to the Himmelraths every month.

I'm not going to have any luck going to the parents, but Jenny and I do have some kind of weird love-hate attraction thing going on, so I guess she's my best hope. It's not a big hope, but still. I call up Tessa and ask, "You got plans for next Saturday?"

"I was thinking of picketing Go Straight to Prom," she says.

"Uh."

"Joke, Lucas. Why, you want to watch movies or something? I just got *Bringing Up Baby*! Katharine Hepburn!"

"Black-and-white and you going goo-goo about your crush all night? Can I ask you something? I mean, if you're attracted to girls and stuff, why can't we watch one of those videos where drunk girls lift their shirts up or something?"

"Lucas. I'm a lesbian. That doesn't mean I'm a man."

"Okay. But listen. I . . . I wanna take you out. I mean, not in a going-out kind of way. But just, like, let's-put-tuxedos-on-and-go-to-the-casino-and-make-fun-of-the-Elvis-impersonator kind of thing. I mean, you've already paid for the tux, right?"

"Yeah. You know what? That sounds awesome."

"Cool."

Okay. So I've got Tessa on board. That was the easy part. The hard part is going to be Jenny Himmelrath.

I find her at her locker the next morning. She's

surrounded by her normal posse. I am not wearing my T-shirt. "Hey, Jenny, can I talk to you?" I say. "Alone?"

"Okay," she says, dismissing her court with a little head gesture. It's kind of amazing.

"Luke," she says. "You know you can't come, right? I mean, maybe before the T-shirts, but my folks won't—"

"I'm actually not here to beg to go to your party." She's startled. No other possibility had occurred to her. "I'm here to beg for something else."

"Luke. Listen, I do like you, and honestly, if it was going to be anybody, it would be you, but I did stand up in church and make a promise that—"

"Gah, that's not it either! Listen. I want to rent the Foot Locker space."

She cocks her head at me. "Well, I mean, just talk to my mom. She—"

"Just for a night. For a party. Next Saturday." I watch as she puts it all together. I figure I need to keep talking before she can voice any objections. "I mean, look, it's not like we want to crash your party, and it's not a protest or any kind of, like, commentary on what you're doing. It's just that we'd like to be able to dance too, you know? That's all. And, I mean, I know that you and Tessa don't—"

"Okay," she says. I was expecting at least fifteen minutes of back and forth before we got to this point, so I'm a little confused.

"Um."

"It'll be easy for me to do it. I know where Mom keeps

the rental agreements, and she's been signing stuff with bands and whatever. It'll be really easy to get her to sign it."

"Wow! Okay, I mean, great! I mean, thanks! I didn't think, I mean, I hoped, obviously, but—"

"I don't want to have to see it, but everybody should have a place to dance. I know you're not evil and I know Tessa's not evil, so you want to have a little party in Foot Locker, go for it. But when people ask you how you got the space, you do not mention my name. Okay?"

"Yeah, fine."

"I'll have the rental agreement for you day after tomorrow."

"Hey, Jenny, thanks. Really. I mean. Well. Have fun at your party."

"You have fun at yours," she says, and then she's gone.

Two days later Jenny slips a piece of paper into my hand. It says we've rented the space for one night for the sum of five hundred dollars. Which is a lot of money. But we'll figure that out later, I guess.

"We got it!" I send to Kate.

"Great," she sends back. "Evites are going out now."

So it's really happening. Tessa Masterson's Big Gay Prom. How's that for a grand gesture?

25

Tessa

This isn't exactly how I pictured this going," my father says. He doesn't—or can't—look right at me so we look at each other in the reflection of his office mirror. To call it an office is sort of an insult to offices worldwide because it's really just a three-quarters-finished porch which means that it's ridiculously hot in the summer, freezing in the winter, and nice in the fall and spring. Tonight is one of those spring nights where you can feel summer tapping you on the shoulder, daring you to imagine swimming in the lake, eating greasy fries at the Shake Shack, or kissing someone before you creep back into your own bedroom. I've imagined all of those things for myself, but I guess I never thought my parents would have imagined them, too.

"So, how did you picture it going?" I ask my dad's reflection.

He shifts in his Teva sandals, absentmindedly picking at a leftover hermit cookie from a Giant Brooks sweets tray. He pauses and for a second I think he'll brush off my question but then, when he puts his hand on my shoulder, I realize he's waiting for me to say it's okay. "Look," I tell him, "I won't be mad. At least, I don't think I will. It's not every day that a girl puts on her best outfit and that outfit has a tie and cumberbund."

Dad cracks a smile. "For starters, I thought I'd give these to Danny." Dad holds out a small green velvet box that has one corner bashed in. "You know my dad didn't have much in the way of stuff. Things. That wasn't where he came from." Dad's cheek has a cookie crumb on it and I focus on that to avoid his eyes. "When your mom and I got married—quickly, I might add—he was already an old man. All hunched over from too many years of lifting bags of concrete."

"This is a really depressing speech to eavesdrop on." Danny clears his throat from the doorway.

I reach for the nearest thing—the rest of the hermit cookie—and chuck it at him and he's gobbled it before my dad's fully registered the intrusion.

"Anyway," Dad says, "my dad was a fighter. Poverty. Hard times. Lack of food stamps."

"Walking to school in the snow uphill both ways," Danny volunteers.

"Danny!" my mom scolds, but it's only halfhearted.

"I know I've told you both this before," Dad goes on, our father-daughter moment now a family one. "But the truth is, I didn't know if I'd be any good at being a father because even though he was a brave guy, a fighter, my dad sort of . . ."

"Sucked?" Danny suggests.

"Wasn't supportive?" I try. Dad nods.

"Yeah, he thought we were nuts to open up a grocery store, wouldn't even sign his name to the bank loan, which made it near impossible to get the initial money."

My mom steps in. "Listen, these kids have a Prom to get to, so let's get to the point." She gives "the look" to my dad, the same one she used when Danny got his sex talk and the same one they exchanged before telling us Grandma Jo had died.

"Did someone die?" Danny asks. At Lucas's suggestion I invited Danny and Anabel to join in our night out so he's in full stud mode, with his tux on, his hair clean and slicked to the side. Danny even smells decent—or rather, he doesn't smell nasty, which is a start.

"No." Dad opens the box. "These were my dad's cuff links, the only decent thing he owned. He gave them to me on my wedding day." Dad's eyes well up with tears and even Danny flinches. "I don't want you to wait that long for my approval, Tessa."

"Dad—" I start, but he unfurls my fingers and puts the box in my right hand.

"You asked and I'll tell you. You were never that little girl who wore a dish towel on her head pretending it was a bridal veil."

"No, that was you, Danny," Mom adds with a smirk.

"And it wasn't like I looked forward to the day some guy would storm in here and take you on a date or anything." Dad wipes the cookie crumb from his face and looks me right in the eyes. "But you do imagine things—like how much you hope your kid is happy in life, finds something to do every day that has some meaning to it. How you hope your kid finds someone to love them as much as you think they're worth." He sucks in a long breath. "And at first, I have to admit this or I'll feel dishonest, at first I was thinking, this is a loss, right? No husband, no bachelor party or what have you. But then I sort of went through all those pictures in my mind—"

"Like a film reel," my mom adds. I picture them up at night, huddled in bed comparing losses.

"And the thing of it is that nowhere in those pictures did I have a man. I suppose I figured it would be a boy, but the reality is it doesn't have to be. And so we made the shirts."

"And we're really behind you one hundred percent," Mom says.

I go to my dad and hug him, the box clenched in my fist. When I pull back, my mom comes over and opens the box with her usual businesslike manner and fixes the cuff links on the French cuff of my fancy white shirt.

The silver and onyx gleam, and when I look in the mirror my whole family is smiling at my reflection—even me.

— — — — — —

I change bags for the eighth time and realize that no matter what kind of purse I bring they all look weird with a tux. Oh well. I take one last look in the mirror as Anabel honks outside. My hair is pulled up in a slouchy-on-purpose bun, with a few wisps at the front so I don't look like a creepy plastic mannequin, and my tuxedo is fantastic, as I thought it would be. I used two oversize safety pins to nip the shirt at the back so it's more fitted, rolled the jacket sleeves a little to showcase the cuff links, and topped the whole look off with some lip gloss, which for me is full makeup. And heels, ones Anabel convinced me to wear. She'd bought them on sale, and shoved wadded-up tissues in the toes because they were too big. "Never pass up a good heel," she'd said. "Because comfort is not the only issue." She removed the tissues so I could fit my feet in, and slid them on, Prince Charming style. I could see why Danny liked her so much. "You're really nice, Anabel." And instead of saying nothing, she looked up at me and said, "And I can see why he tries to do right by you." She'd also instructed me about how to wear my hair so I didn't look "like a creepy ballerina" while telling me about her cousin Greg in Atlanta who'd been living with a guy for a long time.

My heels shine in the porch light.

"Check it out," Danny drawls as we nudge past each other toward the driveway.

"Don't be crass." I laugh and give his arm a quick squeeze as a thanks. "What the—"

"I know!" Danny pumps his fist in the air.

Another honk sounds but it's not from Anabel's dented old Taurus. "A limo?" I ask.

"Don't ask me," Danny says, and rushes for it.

The back tinted window slides down and Anabel, in a sequined strappy dress, sticks half her body out and waves. "Seriously. I had nothing to do with this."

I'm almost to the limo, grin stretching Cadillac-wide on my surprised face, when the back door opens and Lucas steps out. "You want black-and-white-movie glamour? You got it," he says, and reaches for my hand.

"Luke." I say his name and it's so much more than just that. It is thanks and sorry and love all rolled into that sound. "You didn't have to do this."

"Well, I know. But I'm on this no-asshole kick and I kinda like it."

I go with it, nodding and checking out Luke's outfit. "You look like Cary Grant in *The Philadelphia Story*."

"And you're even better looking than Katharine Hepburn."

"Impossible," I say, and we hug, our suits rustling. "Really, Lucas. This is above and beyond the simple night out."

Lucas offers the limo up like it's a prize. "Did I tell you

I'd find a place for us to wear our tuxes?" I nod. "And do I always come through? Don't we always do that for each other?" I wait a few seconds before I respond. And I have my own film reel the way my parents did—me and Lucas crashing our Big Wheels, Lucas running the whole way from Main Street to Giant Brooks because I fell and needed a Band-Aid, Lucas asking me to help him buy the best-smelling deodorant at Hailer's and how we uncapped every single one until I found a brand that didn't make me gag. How we were each other's first and last dance partners at all the school socials just so we didn't have that pressure of finding anyone.

"You're not my fallback, just so you know," I tell him. "Don't think just because I'm not . . . in love with . . ."

"My awesome maleness?"

"Exactly. Just 'cause I'm not in love with you doesn't mean you're not the absolute best thing to ever happen to me."

Lucas tugs me toward the car. It's the first time I've ever been this close to a limo—they don't even have rental companies around here, which means this one must've come from a few counties over. "But see, I realize that my time as the pinnacle of bestness is limited. At some point you'll meet Katharine Hepburn for real . . ."

"First off, she's dead. So eeew. And second, I thought *I* was Katharine Hepburn. Am I dating myself?"

"Can you just turn around and smile so Danny can take our picture and Anabel can hike down her totally inappropriate but totally awesomely short dress?" After a few photos, Lucas holds the door for me and when I slide in, I don't have to worry about my dumb gown or flinch when people compliment me, because I feel so good. Good in my clothing. Good in the car that looks so out of place on our wide rural street, the mailboxes like old clucking hens. Good with my family and Lucas.

And the feeling lasts, even when Luke pins a wilting rose to my lapel, when Danny and Anabel drink from the flask in her bag, and even as we drive the long way through town, past the yacht club with its valet service and lines of cars just like this one.

"Hey, look," I say as our ride zooms past the club, its music audible from here, the limos all in a row. "We blend in."

We get driven to the south side of town, past Giant Brooks and the car dealership out on Second Street with the yellow-and-red flags I always thought looked like a carnival but were just a lame attempt at getting people to buy used vehicles.

At night, with the stores dark and the train tracks empty, the billboards vacant, our town looks really small. And it is. Maybe growing up I didn't realize that, but now I understand it's the kind of place people move away from, and how my parents are different because they came back. And how Luke's mom did, too. And how I might not ever be able to do that because like some old Western shoot-out movie, it might not be a big enough place for me and everyone else.

I look across the limo at Lucas and he's got his arms

stretched out on the seat backs, and my brother's phone is blipping every two seconds, which seems to have Lucas all agitated.

"Don't you think you should answer that?" I ask Danny.

Danny and Anabel are in lip-lock already but take a break so Danny can respond. Lucas gives him a sort of signal.

"What's going on?"

Danny and Lucas have a conversation with gestures the way only guys who run laps and travel for hours to away games can: through gestures and eyebrow raising.

"Ahem, I would like to be clued in here," I say. And then, just to hammer the point home, "Hello? Are we all on Team Tessa or what?"

And as I ask this, the limo slows down.

I put my hand to the window and peer out through the darkened glass. "Do we have a flat?"

There's no other reason to pull into the former Hailer's Drugstore, parking lot of past lives, unless Lucas forget something at home.

But where the Discount LiquorMart once proudly advertised Blue Nun and Pabst, there are no plywood boards covering the storefront.

Instead, there are lights.

And not just any lights. A Hollywood-style spotlight points to the Midwestern sky. Wound together across the entire storefront are multiple strands of purple, red, white, green, blue, and yellow twinkling lights. It's bright. It's slightly tacky. It's a rainbow.

"It's perfect," I say, and open the door so I can get a better look.

Lucas escorts me out of the limousine. When I stand up, Danny claps his hands and from somewhere—I can't see where at first—comes a bellowing noise.

"Is that a tuba?"

"Hooray for sousaphones!" Lucas shouts as the entire marching band from Brookfield-Mason begins to play "Somewhere Over the Rainbow." The music floats down and I realize the band is on the Discount LiquorMart's flat roof, playing just for me.

At what used to be the front door, Ginger Berks from my freshman year Intro to Bio is there, all dressed up and holding a tray of champagne flutes; each glass holds a different-colored liquid to make a rainbow.

"7UP and food coloring," she whispers, and I take a blue glass while walking inside, my eyes wider than ever.

Where the neon letters previously spelled LOWEST PRICES the sign now reads TESSA MASTERSON'S BIG GAY PROM. There are rainbow rubber bracelets with BGP on them. There are lights and cameras and action absolutely everywhere. Most of all, there's me and Lucas.

I turn to him and his eyes are full of the question he asked me, the question that started everything. "You made this happen," I say. And he did. If he hadn't asked me to Prom in the first place, maybe I'd have been one of those people who didn't admit her feelings until college. Or never. Maybe I'd have married a guy just because that's what you do. Or maybe I'd have been fine. Who knows?

"I'd do anything for you," he says, and I know he means it.

"Yes," I tell him, and when he waits I add, "Yes, I will go to Prom with you. And I am so glad you asked."

Lucas gives me his done-good smile and we both check our tuxes. There are tons of people, dancing, swaying, some from school, some are faces I don't know or haven't seen before but probably because they are from out of town. Or perhaps because I stopped looking for the smiles. The crowd seems to wave at us. Then Lucas gives a signal and a former keg—Discount LiquorMart's centerpiece—spouts like a rainbow fountain, and disco balls descend from the ceiling. Glitter actually twinkles down and the Indianapolis Gay Mens' Chorus starts singing.

"Lucas Fogelman, you complete and total asshole," I shout.

"What?" Lucas asks, still holding my hand, and looking worried now.

"You outdid my grand gesture. Now what am I supposed to do?"

Lucas offers his outstretched hand. "Dance?"

And, just like the old us, just like the new us and the future us, we head out on the floor for the first dance, together.

26

LUKE

It's funny. When I imagined this—dancing with Tessa at Prom—it wasn't like this at all. First of all, in my imagination, she was wearing something that at least suggested that she has breasts. But also, when I imagined my hand on her hip, it wasn't just that I imagined something more satiny than a tuxedo under my hand, but I thought the touch would be electric, that it would be the moment when our friendship turned to love.

Dumb ass. It *was* love all along.

Just not, you know, *that* kind of love. This is like dancing with your sister. Or what I imagine dancing with your sister is like. Which is most unlike how Tessa's actual brother is currently dancing with his date. It's really more of a public makeout session than a dance, and it's kind of embarrassing to watch. So I turn away.

And I look at Tessa. I don't know this song that's play-ing. It sounds kind of old, and it's not really the kind of thing I would have chosen if I were the DJ, but I have to admit "You Make Me Feel Brand New" is a pretty good choice. Especially right now, when I'm looking at Tessa, and the singer says "precious friennnnnd . . ."

Tessa's got this big smile on her face and tears are roll-ing down her cheeks, and I feel like I'm going to cry too, but probably for different reasons. Because this song is all about someone who never stopped believing in you, and I did stop believing in her. I failed my best friend, and I have to live with that for the rest of my life.

Or maybe not. Maybe I actually can feel brand new.

"T, I'm so sorry—" I start.

"Lucas. Shut up. I forgave you. Which means you don't have to apologize anymore. You're my best friend. If none of this had ever happened, I wouldn't have all this"—she gestures around at Tessa Masterson's Big Gay Prom—"and I wouldn't . . . oh hell. I can't"—she's getting all choked up now—"this all just means more to me than you can ever know. To be able to really be who I am and have all this too. It's more than I dared to hope for. I started to think being *me* meant giving everything else up." She's really overcome, and she rests her head on my shoulder and just cries for a minute.

We sway to the music, and it's seriously the happiest I've ever been. Maybe I'll get to close out game seven of the World Series, and maybe I won't, but even though nobody's ever going to show highlights of this party on ESPN or even on YouTube, I think maybe this is the best thing I'll ever do.

The song ends, and it kind of breaks the spell. Tessa and I separate and head off the dance floor. And there's Kate Sweeney with a box of tissues that she hands to Tessa, who's still sniffling. "I kinda thought you might need these," she says.

I have to admit, though, that the tissues are not the first things about Kate that I notice. I mean, I've always thought she was pretty, in that girl-next-door way that is pretty irresistible, but she does not look like anybody who lives next door to anybody in Indiana right now. Her long auburn hair is all wavy, and her dress looks like something somebody would wear to the Oscars in the 1940s. Basically she looks like she just stepped out of some classic-movie poster. She's absolutely breathtaking.

And I mean this literally. Like, I can't speak because I can't breathe.

"Y-y-you," I stammer, and Kate flashes me a white-hot smile from between ruby-red lips.

"I thought I would glam it up a little bit," she says.

"I think you succeeded," Tessa says as she tucks a tissue into her pants pocket. "You look like Katharine Hepburn in *The Philadelphia Story*."

"Great movie," Kate says. "But I was aiming for Rita Hayworth."

"Hey," I say, stepping between Tessa and Kate. "Don't even think about it. Tessa's *my* Prom date."

"Hmm . . . ," Kate says. "Ms. Masterson, can I borrow your date for a dance?"

"Wow, Kate, I mean, wow. But I can't really ditch Tessa at her own Prom."

"Yeah, I don't think I'm gonna have a hard time finding somebody to dance with," Tessa says. She gestures at the scene. The dance floor is already full, and people are still streaming in through the front door. There's some up-tempo dance-pop number playing, and the floor is jumping with joyful dancing like I've never seen. Tessa is not the only girl in a tux, but there are also girls in Prom dresses and combat boots, girls in regular Prom dresses, guys in dresses, guys in tuxes, and a fair number of people who are either male or female, but it's not clear from what they're wearing or who they're dancing with.

And, at the wall, there are about forty girls giving Tessa that I'm-trying-to-get-up-the-courage-to-ask-you-to-dance look. She smiles. "You kids have fun," she says, but then turns to Kate. "But I get him back for the last dance. And since this is my Big Gay Prom, I am not letting this night go by without a dance with the glamorous movie star," she says.

"Deal," Kate says, and Tessa evaporates into the crowd.

Which leaves me alone with Kate Sweeney. "Um, so, will you dance with me?" I say.

"I seriously thought you'd never ask," she says, smiling again.

Just then the up-tempo song ends, and the DJ slows it down. And now I'm slow dancing with a movie star, and my hand on her hip feels like something more intimate than you should be allowed to do in public.

"Thank you," I whisper in her ear. "This is perfect. It's better than perfect." I look around at the other couples on the floor. I wonder how many of these people, like Danny Masterson, probably could have gone to any Prom, and how many, like this skinny kid next to me with his arms around the neck of a big chubby guy, thought they'd never get to do anything like this—that Prom was something for other kids.

"Where did all these people come from?" I ask.

"I put it out on pretty much every Facebook group I could think of," Kate says. "I think pretty much every gay and lesbian kid in Indiana got the message. Twenty bucks a head, so we can cover the rent. And now you're going to shut up about the logistics of this Prom and let me enjoy slow dancing with a hot guy."

I look around to see which hot guy she's referring to, and she punches me, and I pull her close, and I think, so this is what magic feels like. I don't really plan this, but I can't help it. If I don't kiss her right now, I'm going to go completely insane. So I do. But not quickly this time. And once I start, it's not that easy to stop.

I really hate kids who make out on the dance floor. Or

I used to, anyway, before I became one. The song ends, and suddenly Tessa comes over and breaks us up. "Don't make me call the chaperone," Tessa says.

Kate smiles at me. "To be continued," she says.

She and Tessa go off and shake it to some Miss Kaboom song, and then Tessa grabs me for a dance. It's another high-energy song, and I know Tessa is my best friend because she doesn't mock me for being a really terrible dancer.

And the party goes on and on. I pretty much never stop dancing. With Tessa, with Kate, with some random guy in a pink dress who is probably the best dancer in the room and who slips his number into my palm when the dance is over.

About two hours later, my jacket, like most of the tuxedo jackets, is in a heap on the floor somewhere, and I'm sweaty and exhausted and happy. Since this was a retail space, it has air-conditioning, but this system was never meant to counteract summer heat and hundreds of dancing teenagers.

"I need a break," I say to Kate, after another slow dance, and, arm around her waist, I lead her off the dance floor. Over at the door, a big muscular guy in a suit with sunglasses on—inside, after dark—is talking to the kid selling tickets. He scans the floor and points at Kate, who says to me, "Wow. I think . . . Well, let me just go talk to that guy."

She leaves me standing there while she talks to the

gigantic dude who, with my luck, is probably her jealous ex. Suddenly Tessa is standing there.

"Hey!" I say. "Having fun?"

"Seriously the best night of my life," she says, smiling. Then she follows my gaze to the door, where there are now three huge guys in suits and sunglasses. "Um. What's that? Are they shutting us down?"

"Those are definitely not Brookfield cops," I say. "I honestly have no idea what's happening."

Tessa looks worried. I feel worried. As innocent as this event is, I'm sure there are people full of hate who might have a violent objection to it happening. I didn't even give a thought to security.

Kate comes walking back with a huge smile on her face. "Awesome," she says. "It was a long shot, and I totally did it for a gag, but it's really happening!"

"Kate, what the hell are you talking about?"

"You'll see," she says.

Several more big dudes enter and stand at the front of the room by the DJ and stare, blank-faced, at the crowd.

The music keeps playing, but the crowd thins out as it becomes impossible to ignore the fact that there's more musical equipment being set up at the front of the room. Two more colossal stacks of speakers appear next to the DJ's speakers. A bass player, a guitar player, a drummer, and two keyboard players appear, looking a little cramped in the back of a former Foot Locker.

I'm standing in a crowd with Kate, Tessa, Danny,

Anabel, and what seems like every girl Tessa's danced with all night. It's a big crowd. "Seriously," I say to Kate, "you have to tell me what's going on."

Kate has this gigantic grin plastered on her face. "You'll see. Really soon."

And sure enough, at that point the drummer unleashes a big drumroll that causes even the few diehards on the dance floor to stop and look. At the back of the room, there's some commotion, and four more colossal, muscular guys come in. Only these guys are not wearing suits and sunglasses. They're wearing black Speedos and what seems to be a thin coating of oil. And they're carrying something between them. A big litter with what looks like a giant, closed-up flower in the middle.

"No way," I say, looking at Kate. "No way. This is not happening."

"She lives in Chicago. I sent an Evite through her Facebook page. I didn't think she'd actually show up!" Kate says.

The crowd is buzzing like none of them can believe it either.

The oiled musclemen stop in front of the band and set their burden down.

And just like at the Grammys, one petal of the flower peels down and Top-40 dance diva Miss Kaboom steps out. Her long blond hair shoots up from her head, bride-of-Frankenstein style, she's got a slash of red makeup across her eyes, and she's wearing thigh-high boots with a black bikini bottom, but instead of whatever scraps of fabric might usually be on her top half, she's wearing, I swear to God, a TEAM TESSA T-shirt.

Hundreds of cell phones appear in the screaming crowd, snapping pictures and taking videos. Maybe they really will be showing highlights from this for years. She strides to the microphone and grabs it like it owes her money.

"Somebody told me there was a Big Gay Prom here tonight!" she shouts, and the entire crowd, the big, sweaty room full of gay kids, straight kids, bi kids, trans kids, unsure kids, band geeks, theater fags, drag queens and kings, kids who, for whatever reason, feel like they don't fit in anywhere—in other words, teenagers—roars.

"Where's Tessa?" Miss Kaboom shouts, and Tessa, blushing so hard she's purple, walks up to the band.

"Can I have this dance?" Miss Kaboom asks, and Tessa nods.

"Cool! All right, gay Indiana, bi Indiana, trans Indiana, straight Indiana! Are you ready to party?"

And the crowd roars again.

"This isn't one of my songs, but I thought it was appropriate. Happy Prom night!" The guitarist starts playing this chunka-chunka-chunka riff, the rest of the band kicks in, and Miss Kaboom is singing about wanting the world to know and letting it show, and she and Tessa are dancing, and so is everybody else. Including my mom. Well, we're the only people who live on this block, and with this noise, there was no way she was going to sleep. At a normal Prom, I'd be horrified to see my mom on the dance floor. But here, it kind of feels okay. She looks over at me and points at Miss Kaboom with a can-you-believe-this? expression on her face. I give her a big thumbs-up, and she melts into the crowd.

When the song finishes, Tessa comes over and gives me a big hug. "This is just the best thing ever," she says. "I never want this night to end!"

Neither do I. Tomorrow everybody here has to go back to real life, which isn't always as welcoming and fun as an abandoned Foot Locker with a Big Gay Prom in it. Some will go back to families, communities, or high schools that don't accept them for who they are. Some will go back to people who want them to know for sure who they are before they're ready to make that call. Some will go back into hiding.

But I hope that even more of them will be like Tessa and get to wake up tomorrow feeling like it's okay to be themselves. I guess for the first time since I asked Tessa to Prom, I feel kind of hopeful. At the Go Straight to Prom, the DJ will be playing Miss Kaboom's "Shake It," which, by the way, Miss Kaboom is playing live right in front of us while several hundred people shake it like they think they might never get to shake it again.

I guess it's kind of sad that we had to have this event in the first place, and that so many people here felt like they couldn't just be who they are at their own Proms. We shouldn't have to dance separately.

But, I mean, at least we're dancing to the same music. And that has to count for something.

After what seems like hours on the dance floor, Miss Kaboom announces, "All right. Last dance, everybody. Even Miss Kaboom needs to sleep sometime!"

Tessa comes over and grabs me from Kate. "Sorry, glamour girl," she says, and takes me to the dance floor as Miss Kaboom fires up "Isla de Amor," which seems to be her only slow song.

"I'm gonna have to insist that you stop flirting with my girlfriend," I say.

"Look who's got a girlfriend!" Tessa says.

"Well. I mean, yeah. But she's totally cool, you know, she's not gonna be all, why are you getting texts from Tessa and stuff. You know?"

"Will you shut up and dance?" Tessa says, so I do.

And when the dance is over and everybody's slowly filing out, I'm standing there with Tessa, Kate, Danny, and Anabel. Mom comes over and says, "Who wants breakfast?"

Kate leans over and whispers in my ear, "That's not really the post-Prom tradition I was hoping to observe, but I guess we'll have plenty of time when we have dorm rooms. I've got a single next year," she says, and it's all I can do to remain conscious.

When I recover, I find that I'm actually starving from dancing all night, so we go upstairs and, as the morning sun breaks through the windows, we devour enough pancakes to feed most of Brookfield on a normal day.

And then I'm tired. Danny and Anabel head out, Kate gives me a luscious kiss good-bye, and I'm sitting there with just Tessa.

"Well, I'm beat," I say.

"Not me," Tessa says. "Come on. Grab a ball and a couple of gloves, and let's go."

"Come on, Tessa. I'm completely beat. Let's get a couple of hours of—" I see the look on her face and stop. "All right. I've gotta change, though. I can't pitch in a tux. Gimme five minutes."

And so, twenty minutes later, we're back where it all began, behind the loading dock at Giant Brooks. Like I've done a million times, I'm throwing to Tessa, who's crouched down in a catcher's position. She flashes a hand signal.

"Come on, T, not the circle change again," I complain.

"Lucas. You've gotta get that pitch down."

"Yeah, well, maybe I might do a little better at it when I've slept some time in the last day!" I say.

Tessa flashes an evil grin. "Not interested in your excuses, rookie. Just throw the ball."

I unleash the circle change, and, finally, for the first time this morning, the ball floats down and in, probably at least ten miles an hour slower than my fastball.

"That's what I'm talking about!" Tessa says. "That's a swinging strike or maybe a groundout every time. Now do it again."

"You are killing me here," I say. And I do it again.

"Strike two!" she cries. "Now bring the heat!"

Maybe it's just because I'm sleep deprived, but this suddenly gets to me. I remember being ten years old back here with Tessa shouting at me to bring the heat, back when the heat was a "fast" ball that was slower than my slowest off-speed pitch is today. It's like nothing has changed, and everything has changed, and it just suddenly feels overwhelming.

"T," I say. "Are we gonna . . . like when we go to college and you're busy and famous—"

"Who says I'm gonna be famous?"

"T, you're the best-known lesbian in the Midwest. I think you're gonna be a celebrity at Northwestern."

She smiles. "I don't know if I'm gonna do any more interviews, though. It's exhausting. But if my current celebrity status gets me some dates, I guess that'll be okay."

I can't help laughing. I've talked about my dates a lot with her, but she never reciprocated, and I never really knew why. It's like I'm finally seeing Tessa for who she is, or maybe she's just finally showing me her whole self.

"But so, when you're, like, studying all the time and being a big stud on campus—" I start.

"I can't be a stud," she says. "That's a male thing."

"So what's the female equivalent?" I ask.

"There isn't one. Not one that expresses admiration the way 'stud' does."

"How about 'heartbreaker'?"

Tessa thinks for a second. "It's not perfect, but I'll take it. But you were saying. When I'm a heartbreaker making the dean's list, are we still gonna call each other? Are we still gonna be friends? Will I drive to Purdue to help you with your circle change? Stuff like that?"

"Yeah. I guess that's what I was going to say, more or less."

"Lucas. Our friendship survived a doomed crush, a media firestorm, and a Big Gay Prom. What the hell makes you think it can't survive college?"

"I dunno. I guess most people don't stay friends, or they grow apart or something."

"Well, in case you haven't noticed," she says, "we're not most people. Now are you gonna bring the heat, or do I call for a reliever?"

"I'm bringing the heat," I say. I wind up and give her the best fastball I've got.

It hits her glove with a slap you could probably hear all the way in Mason.

"Strike three! And damn, that hurts like hell!" she says, popping her hand out of the glove and shaking it back and forth. "You must really want to get out of here, huh?"

The funny thing is, I don't. I'm in the sunshine playing catch with my best friend. Why would I want to be anywhere else?

"If you can't handle catching me anymore, I totally get it. I mean, you are just a girl," I say.

Tessa picks up the glove and puts it back on. "So that's how it is, huh? Okay, tough guy, gimme the circle change again."

LUKE

I'm in the zone with the circle change. I watch as it leaves my hand, flies straight, and dives across the plate at the last second.

Tessa smiles. "Perfect," she says.

TESSA MASTERSON GOES TO PROM
By Cindy Alpert
Brookfield-Mason Regional

Brookfield was stunned on Saturday as pop star Miss Kaboom (real name Melissa Kabagleon) made a surprise appearance at an event on Brookfield's south side called Tessa Masterson's Big Gay Prom. This event, planned in the aftermath of the school board's cancellation of the official Prom, drew partygoers from three states.

Prior to Miss Kaboom's appearance, the event was a regular teen dance, unremarkable except for the number of same-sex couples on the dance floor and the rainbow lights.

In an exclusive interview with the *Bee*, Miss Kaboom revealed the reason for her visit. "I was invited," she said. Asked what she thought of the event, Miss Kaboom said, "I have partied with the richest, most famous people on four continents. And I have honestly never had as much fun as I did tonight. I'm writing a song about it. Look for it on my next album."

In an exclusive interview with the *Bee*, Tessa Masterson had this to say: "I am the luckiest person in the whole world. I have people in my life who love me because of who I am, not in spite of it. And, I mean, look, I might be a lesbian, but I did grow up here. I think every girl in Brookfield imagines that Prom will be the best night of her life. And for me, it was. So far."

Asked what could possibly top a party bearing her name, with a celebrity guest star, Tessa had this to say: "My wedding day. I mean, not that I have any candidates right now, but when I can legally marry the woman I love on the front steps of Brookfield Town Hall, that will be the best day of my life. Everybody will be invited. And I already know who my best man will be."

Acknowledgments

Thanks to Brendan Halpin, Faye and Doug, Emily and the crew at Bloomsbury, Adam and the offspring, Hooter von Binken. My seven-year-old daughter said, "Wouldn't it be great if people could just love whoever they want and people could just be happy for them?" —E. F.
www.emilyfranklin.com
www.wellcookedlife.com

Brendan thanks Suzanne, Casey, Rowen, Kylie, and Cooper. Thanks also to Emily Franklin, Doug Stewart, Emily Easton, and Miss Kaboom. Thanks to the state of Massachusetts for equal marriage. Thanks to Dan Savage and the It Gets Better Project: www.itgetsbetter.org —B. H.
www.brendanhalpin.com